# MARVEL

# MARVEL ACTION

# SPIDER-MAN

## SHOCK TO THE SYSTEM

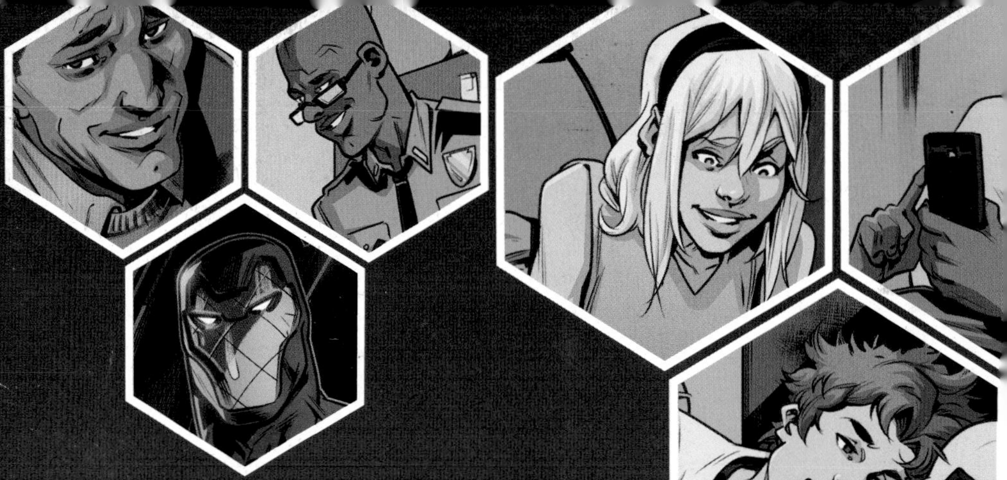

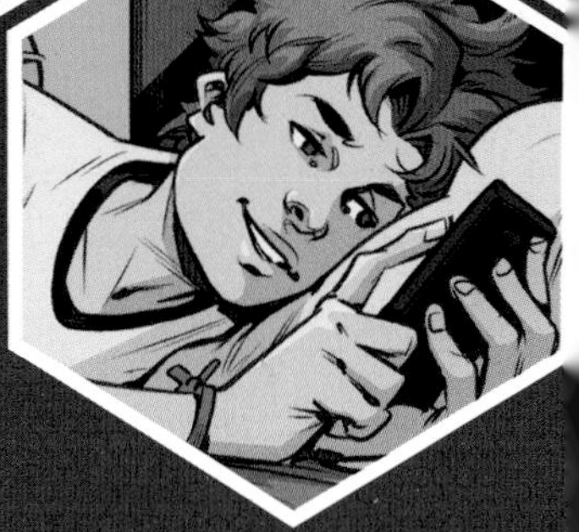


**Marvel Publishing:**

**Jeff Youngquist:** VP Production & Special Projects
**Lauren Bisom:** Editor, Juvenile Publishing
**Caitlin O'Connell:** Assistant Editor, Special Projects
**Sven Larsen:** Director, Licensed Publishing
**David Gabriel:** SVP Print, Sales & Marketing
**C.B. Cebulski:** Editor-In-Chief
**Joe Quesada:** Chief Creative Officer
**Dan Buckley:** President, Marvel Entertainment
**Alan Fine:** Executive Producer

**IDW Publishing:**

IDW

Cover Art by
FICO OSSIO

Collection Edits by
ALONZO SIMON
and ZAC BOONE

Collection Production by
SHAWN LEE

Jerry Bennington, President
Nachie Marshum, Publisher
Cara Morrison, Chief Financial Officer
Matthew Ruzicka, Chief Accounting Officer
Rebekah Cahalin, EVP of Operations
John Barber, Editor-in-Chief
Justin Eisinger, Editorial Director, Graphic Novels & Collections
Scott Dunbier, Director, Special Projects
Blake Kobashigawa, VP of Sales
Lorelei Bunjes, VP of Technology & Information Services
Anna Morrow, Sr Marketing Director
Tara McCrillis, Director of Design & Production
Mike Ford, Director of Operations
Shauna Monteforte, Manufacturing Operations Director
Ted Adams and Robbie Robbins, IDW Founders

ISBN: 978-1-68405-720-7     23 22 21 20     1 2 3 4

Special thanks: **Nick Lowe**





Printed in Korea.

Originally published as MARVEL ACTION: SPIDER-MAN, VOL. 2 #1–3.

# MARVEL ACTION
# SPIDER-MAN

## SHOCK TO THE SYSTEM

WRITTEN BY **BRANDON EASTON**

ART BY **FICO OSSIO**

COLORS BY **RONDA PATTISON**

LETTERS BY **SHAWN LEE**

EDITORIAL ASSISTANT **RILEY FARMER**

EDITORS **ELIZABETH BREI & CHASE MAROTZ**

SPIDER-MAN CREATED BY
**STAN LEE & STEVE DITKO**

# PART ONE

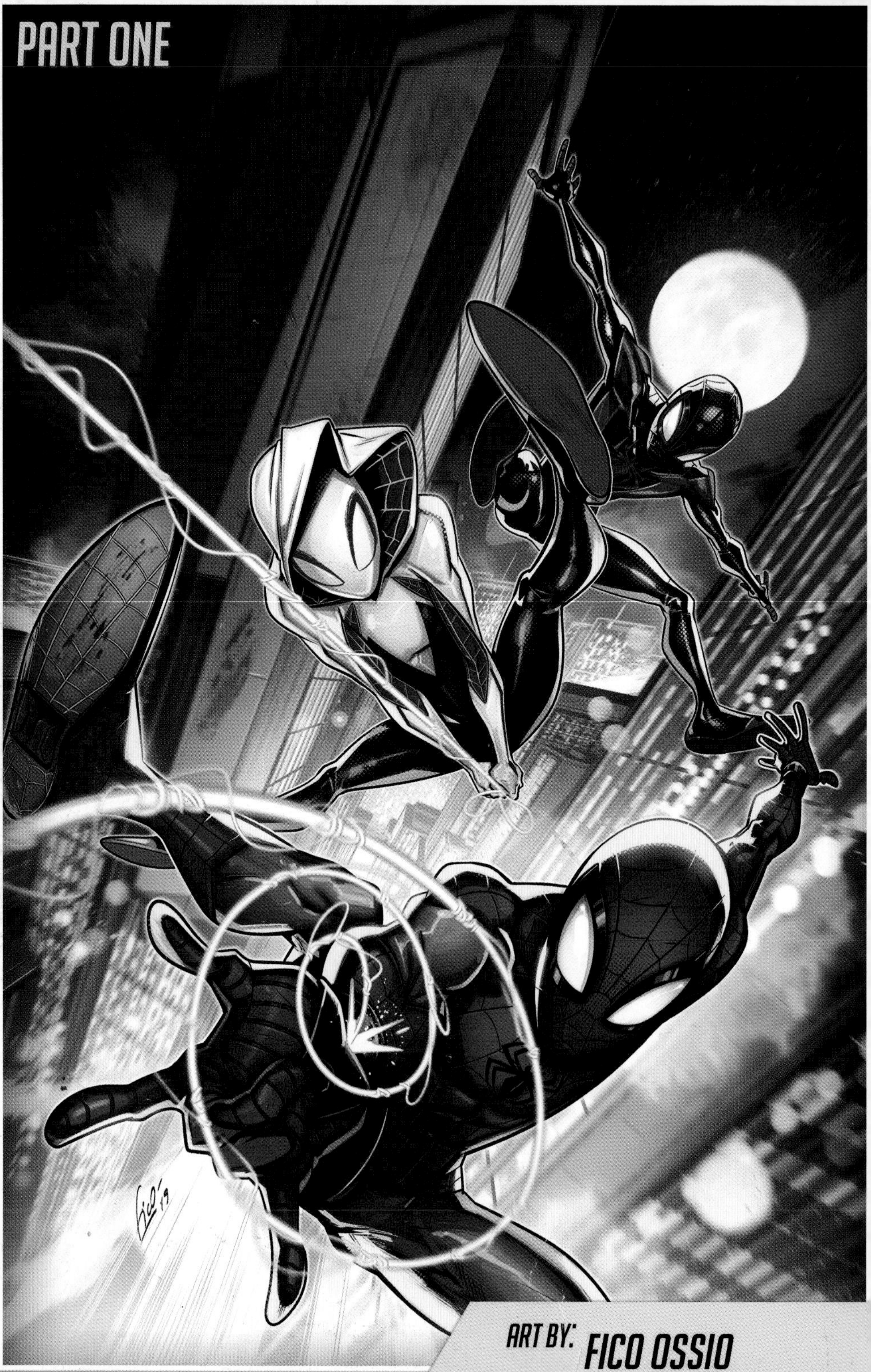

ART BY: FICO OSSIO

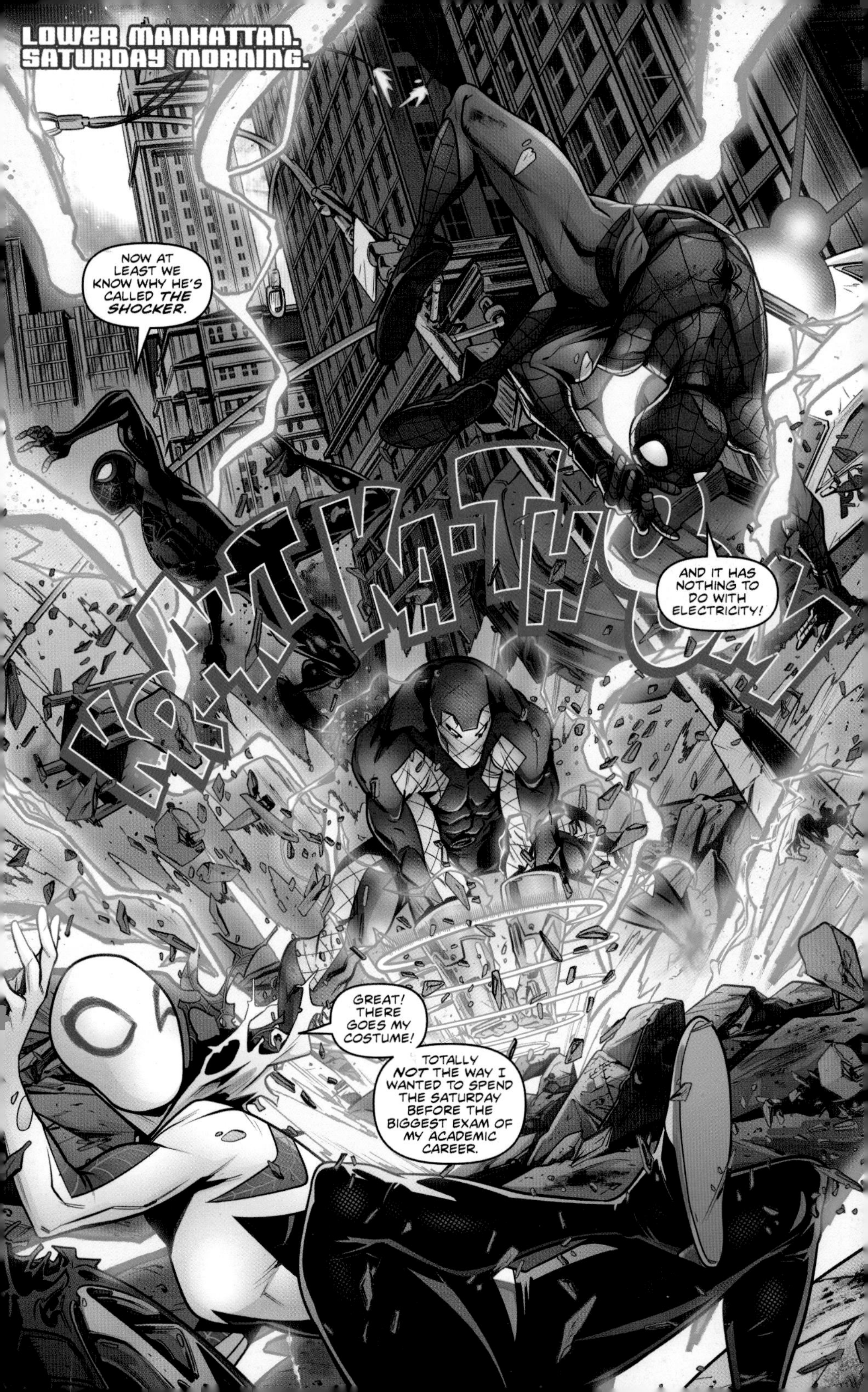
LOWER MANHATTAN.
SATURDAY MORNING.
NOW AT LEAST WE KNOW WHY HE'S CALLED *THE SHOCKER*.
AND IT HAS NOTHING TO DO WITH ELECTRICITY!
KA-THOOM
GREAT! THERE GOES MY COSTUME!
TOTALLY *NOT* THE WAY I WANTED TO SPEND THE SATURDAY BEFORE THE BIGGEST EXAM OF MY ACADEMIC CAREER.

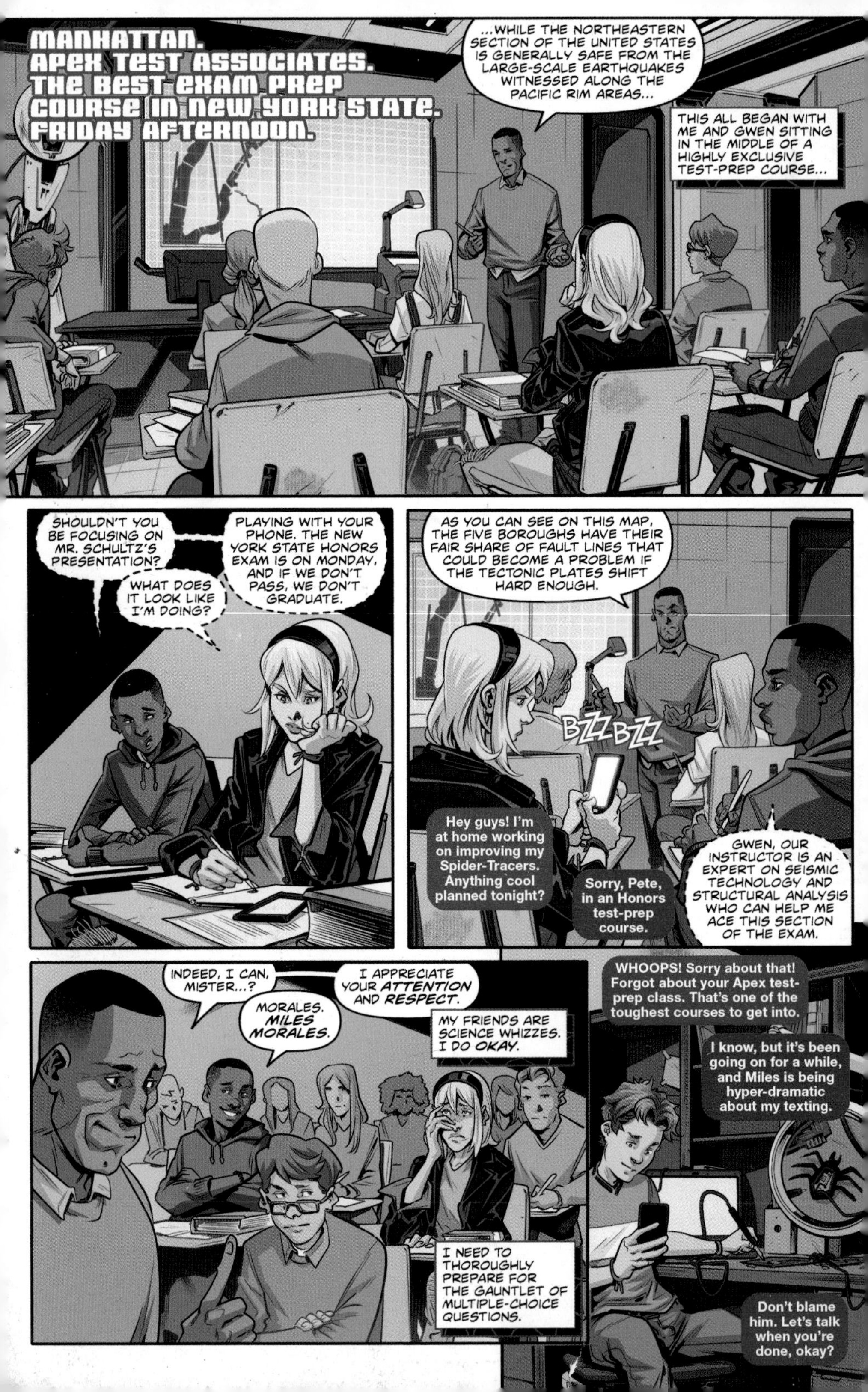

MANHATTAN. APEX TEST ASSOCIATES. THE BEST EXAM PREP COURSE IN NEW YORK STATE. FRIDAY AFTERNOON.
...WHILE THE NORTHEASTERN SECTION OF THE UNITED STATES IS GENERALLY SAFE FROM THE LARGE-SCALE EARTHQUAKES WITNESSED ALONG THE PACIFIC RIM AREAS...
THIS ALL BEGAN WITH ME AND GWEN SITTING IN THE MIDDLE OF A HIGHLY EXCLUSIVE TEST-PREP COURSE...
SHOULDN'T YOU BE FOCUSING ON MR. SCHULTZ'S PRESENTATION?
WHAT DOES IT LOOK LIKE I'M DOING?
PLAYING WITH YOUR PHONE. THE NEW YORK STATE HONORS EXAM IS ON MONDAY, AND IF WE DON'T PASS, WE DON'T GRADUATE.
AS YOU CAN SEE ON THIS MAP, THE FIVE BOROUGHS HAVE THEIR FAIR SHARE OF FAULT LINES THAT COULD BECOME A PROBLEM IF THE TECTONIC PLATES SHIFT HARD ENOUGH.
BZZZ BZZZ
Hey guys! I'm at home working on improving my Spider-Tracers. Anything cool planned tonight?
Sorry, Pete, in an Honors test-prep course.
GWEN, OUR INSTRUCTOR IS AN EXPERT ON SEISMIC TECHNOLOGY AND STRUCTURAL ANALYSIS WHO CAN HELP ME ACE THIS SECTION OF THE EXAM.
INDEED, I CAN, MISTER...?
MORALES. MILES MORALES.
I APPRECIATE YOUR ATTENTION AND RESPECT.
MY FRIENDS ARE SCIENCE WHIZZES. I DO OKAY.
I NEED TO THOROUGHLY PREPARE FOR THE GAUNTLET OF MULTIPLE-CHOICE QUESTIONS.
WHOOPS! Sorry about that! Forgot about your Apex test-prep class. That's one of the toughest courses to get into.
I know, but it's been going on for a while, and Miles is being hyper-dramatic about my texting.
Don't blame him. Let's talk when you're done, okay?

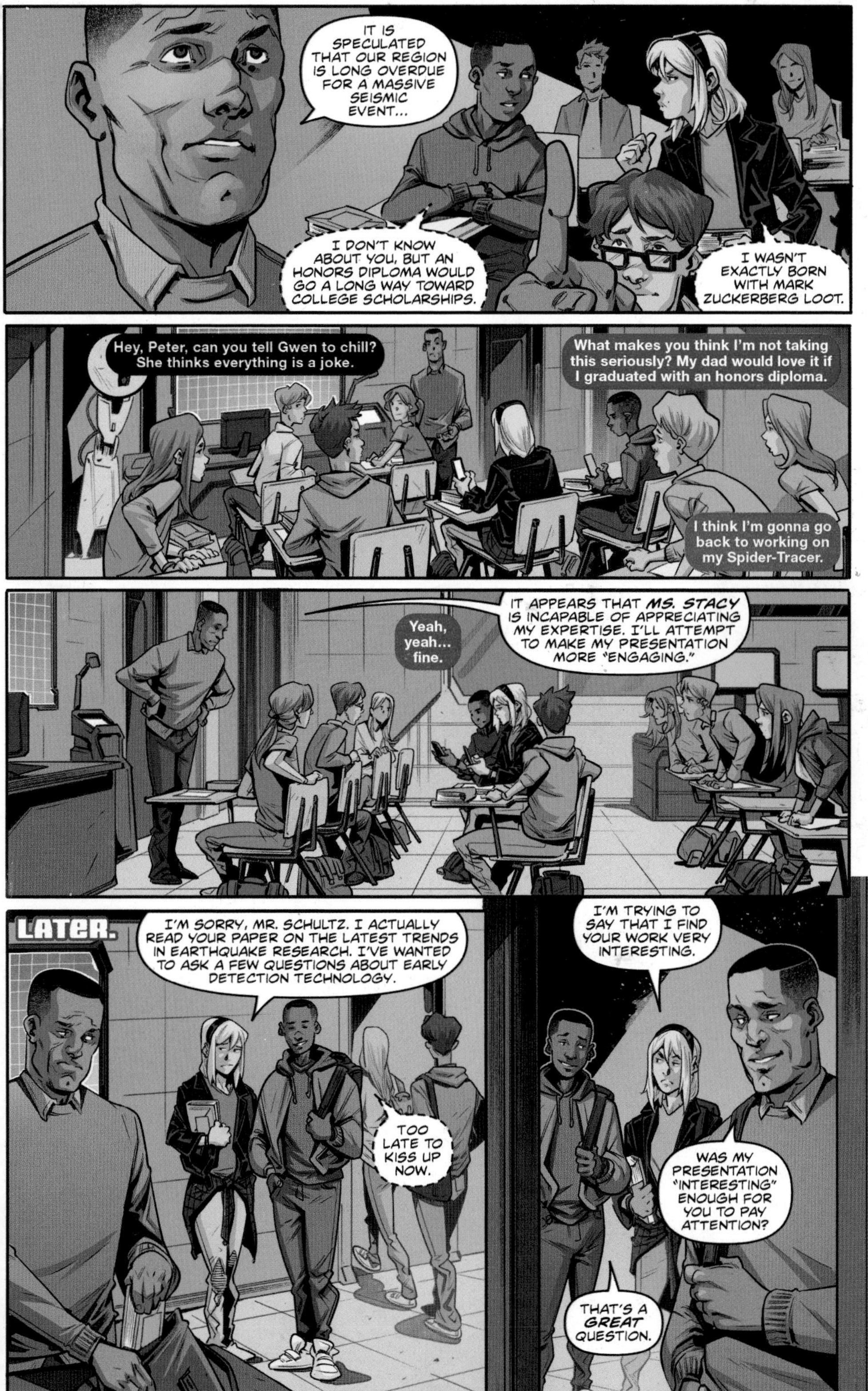
IT IS SPECULATED THAT OUR REGION IS LONG OVERDUE FOR A MASSIVE SEISMIC EVENT...
I DON'T KNOW ABOUT YOU, BUT AN HONORS DIPLOMA WOULD GO A LONG WAY TOWARD COLLEGE SCHOLARSHIPS.
I WASN'T EXACTLY BORN WITH MARK ZUCKERBERG LOOT.
Hey, Peter, can you tell Gwen to chill? She thinks everything is a joke.
What makes you think I'm not taking this seriously? My dad would love it if I graduated with an honors diploma.
I think I'm gonna go back to working on my Spider-Tracer.
Yeah, yeah... fine.
IT APPEARS THAT MS. STACY IS INCAPABLE OF APPRECIATING MY EXPERTISE. I'LL ATTEMPT TO MAKE MY PRESENTATION MORE "ENGAGING."
LATER.
I'M SORRY, MR. SCHULTZ. I ACTUALLY READ YOUR PAPER ON THE LATEST TRENDS IN EARTHQUAKE RESEARCH. I'VE WANTED TO ASK A FEW QUESTIONS ABOUT EARLY DETECTION TECHNOLOGY.
TOO LATE TO KISS UP NOW.
I'M TRYING TO SAY THAT I FIND YOUR WORK VERY INTERESTING.
WAS MY PRESENTATION "INTERESTING" ENOUGH FOR YOU TO PAY ATTENTION?
THAT'S A GREAT QUESTION.

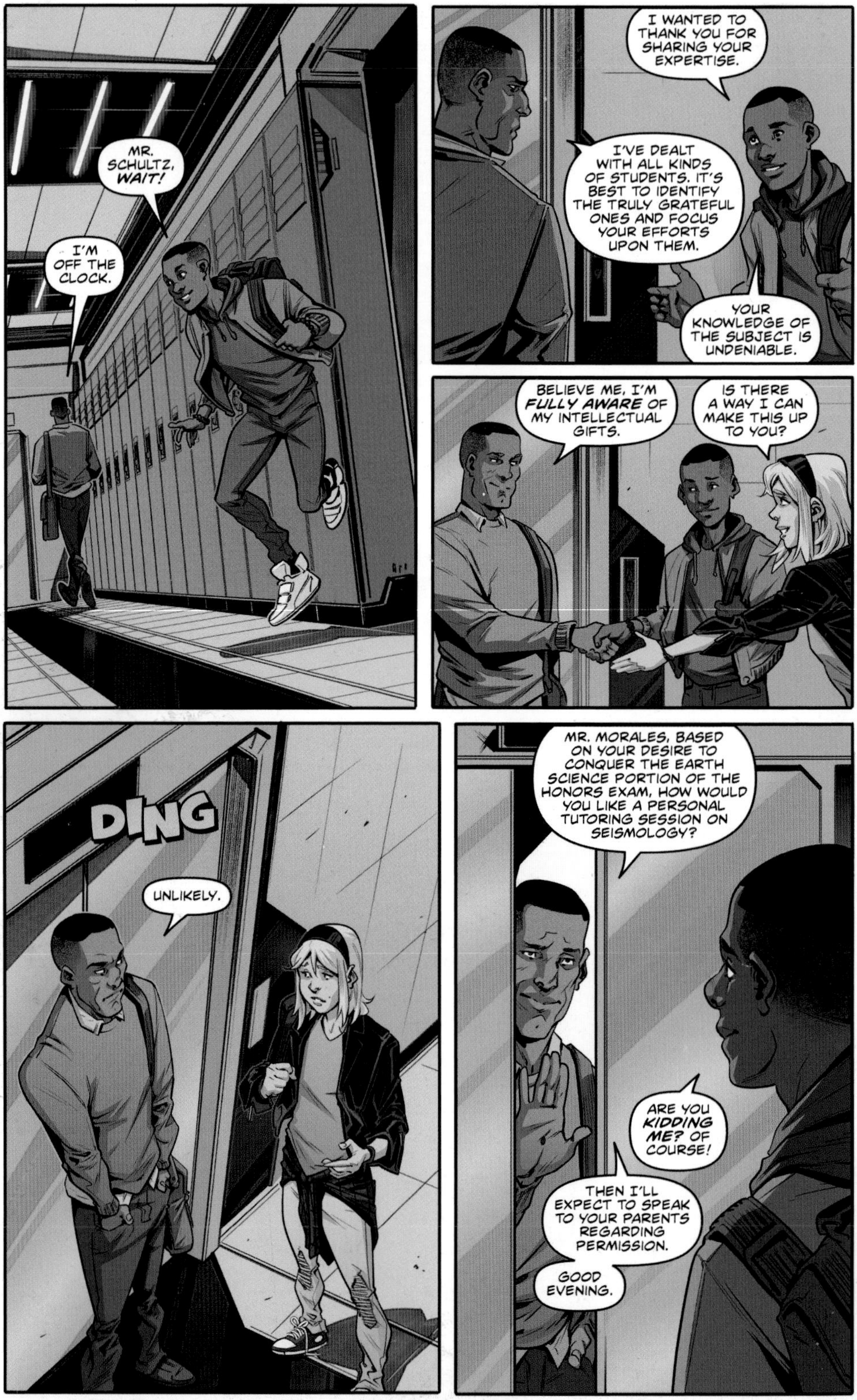
MR. SCHULTZ, WAIT!
I'M OFF THE CLOCK.
I WANTED TO THANK YOU FOR SHARING YOUR EXPERTISE.
I'VE DEALT WITH ALL KINDS OF STUDENTS. IT'S BEST TO IDENTIFY THE TRULY GRATEFUL ONES AND FOCUS YOUR EFFORTS UPON THEM.
YOUR KNOWLEDGE OF THE SUBJECT IS UNDENIABLE.
BELIEVE ME, I'M FULLY AWARE OF MY INTELLECTUAL GIFTS.
IS THERE A WAY I CAN MAKE THIS UP TO YOU?
DING
UNLIKELY.
MR. MORALES, BASED ON YOUR DESIRE TO CONQUER THE EARTH SCIENCE PORTION OF THE HONORS EXAM, HOW WOULD YOU LIKE A PERSONAL TUTORING SESSION ON SEISMOLOGY?
ARE YOU KIDDING ME? OF COURSE!
THEN I'LL EXPECT TO SPEAK TO YOUR PARENTS REGARDING PERMISSION.
GOOD EVENING.

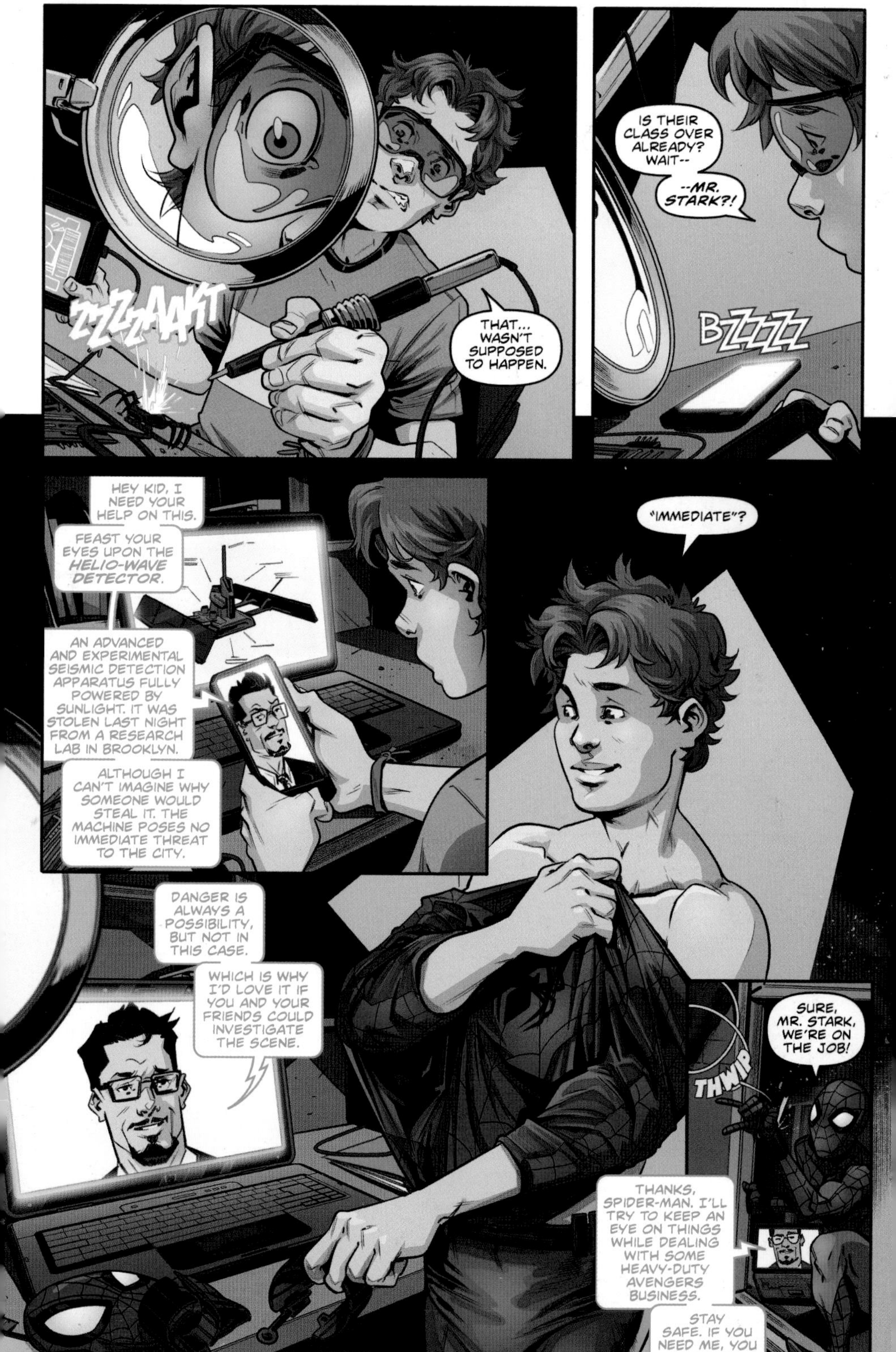
ZZZZAAKT
THAT... WASN'T SUPPOSED TO HAPPEN.
BZZZZ
IS THEIR CLASS OVER ALREADY? WAIT--
--MR. STARK?!
HEY KID, I NEED YOUR HELP ON THIS.
FEAST YOUR EYES UPON THE HELIO-WAVE DETECTOR.
AN ADVANCED AND EXPERIMENTAL SEISMIC DETECTION APPARATUS FULLY POWERED BY SUNLIGHT. IT WAS STOLEN LAST NIGHT FROM A RESEARCH LAB IN BROOKLYN.
ALTHOUGH I CAN'T IMAGINE WHY SOMEONE WOULD STEAL IT. THE MACHINE POSES NO IMMEDIATE THREAT TO THE CITY.
"IMMEDIATE"?
DANGER IS ALWAYS A POSSIBILITY, BUT NOT IN THIS CASE.
WHICH IS WHY I'D LOVE IT IF YOU AND YOUR FRIENDS COULD INVESTIGATE THE SCENE.
THWIP
SURE, MR. STARK, WE'RE ON THE JOB!
THANKS, SPIDER-MAN. I'LL TRY TO KEEP AN EYE ON THINGS WHILE DEALING WITH SOME HEAVY-DUTY AVENGERS BUSINESS.
STAY SAFE. IF YOU NEED ME, YOU KNOW HOW TO FIND ME.

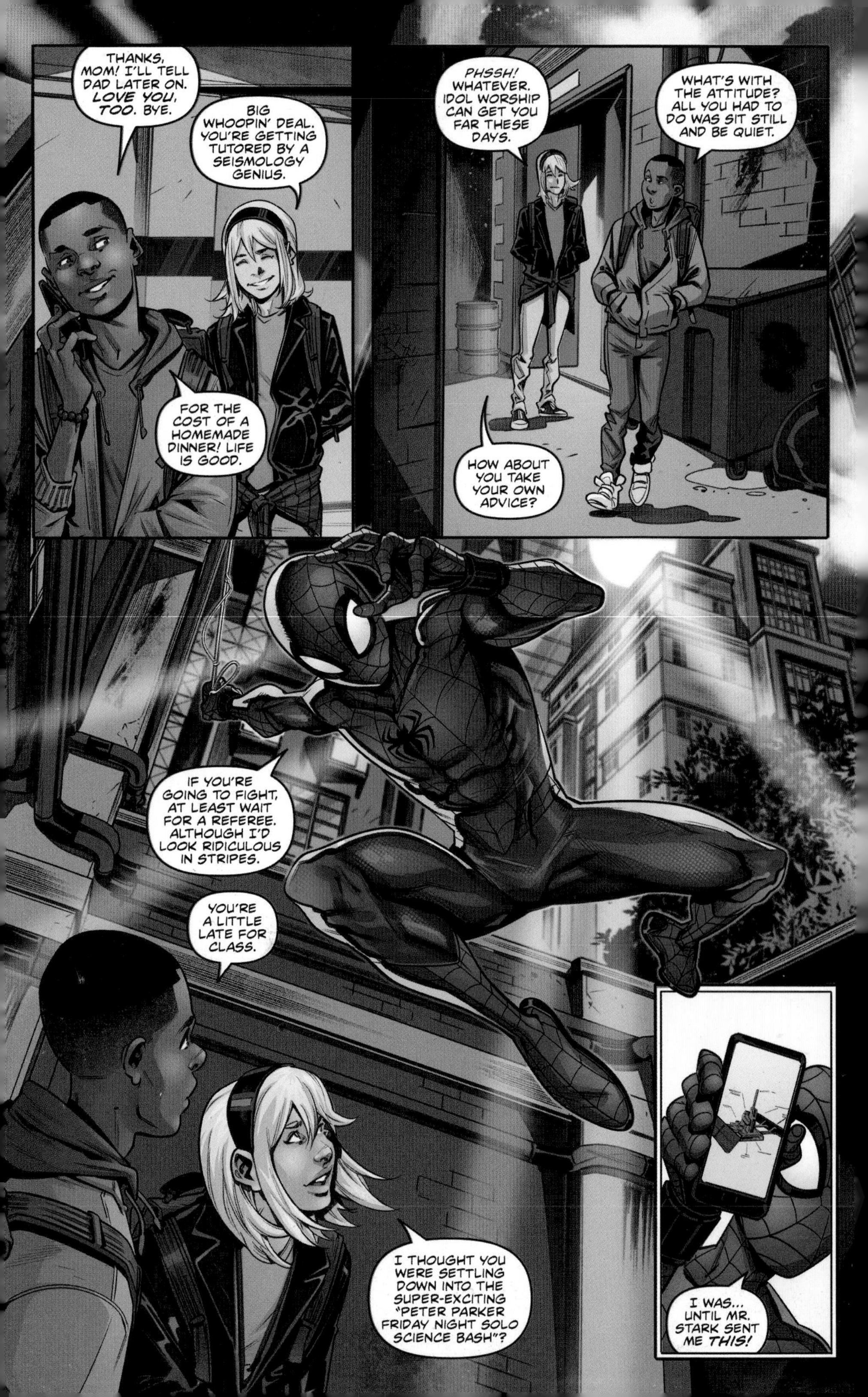
THANKS, MOM! I'LL TELL DAD LATER ON. LOVE YOU, TOO. BYE.
BIG WHOOPIN' DEAL. YOU'RE GETTING TUTORED BY A SEISMOLOGY GENIUS.
FOR THE COST OF A HOMEMADE DINNER! LIFE IS GOOD.
PHSSH! WHATEVER. IDOL WORSHIP CAN GET YOU FAR THESE DAYS.
WHAT'S WITH THE ATTITUDE? ALL YOU HAD TO DO WAS SIT STILL AND BE QUIET.
HOW ABOUT YOU TAKE YOUR OWN ADVICE?
IF YOU'RE GOING TO FIGHT, AT LEAST WAIT FOR A REFEREE. ALTHOUGH I'D LOOK RIDICULOUS IN STRIPES.
YOU'RE A LITTLE LATE FOR CLASS.
I THOUGHT YOU WERE SETTLING DOWN INTO THE SUPER-EXCITING "PETER PARKER FRIDAY NIGHT SOLO SCIENCE BASH"?
I WAS... UNTIL MR. STARK SENT ME THIS!

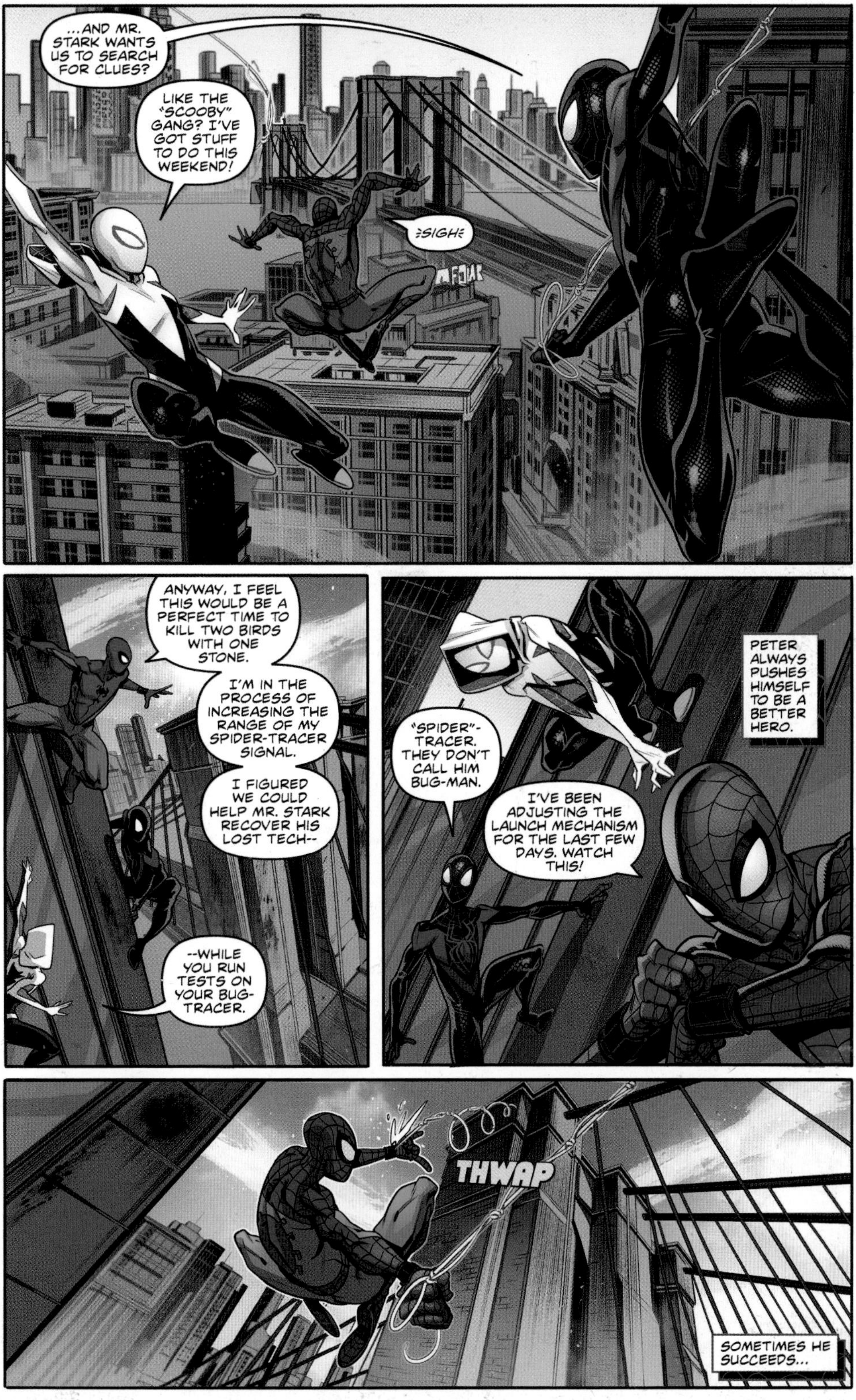
...AND MR. STARK WANTS US TO SEARCH FOR CLUES?
LIKE THE "SCOOBY" GANG? I'VE GOT STUFF TO DO THIS WEEKEND!
SIGH
ANYWAY, I FEEL THIS WOULD BE A PERFECT TIME TO KILL TWO BIRDS WITH ONE STONE.
I'M IN THE PROCESS OF INCREASING THE RANGE OF MY SPIDER-TRACER SIGNAL.
I FIGURED WE COULD HELP MR. STARK RECOVER HIS LOST TECH--
--WHILE YOU RUN TESTS ON YOUR BUG-TRACER.
PETER ALWAYS PUSHES HIMSELF TO BE A BETTER HERO.
"SPIDER"-TRACER. THEY DON'T CALL HIM BUG-MAN.
I'VE BEEN ADJUSTING THE LAUNCH MECHANISM FOR THE LAST FEW DAYS. WATCH THIS!
THWAP
SOMETIMES HE SUCCEEDS...

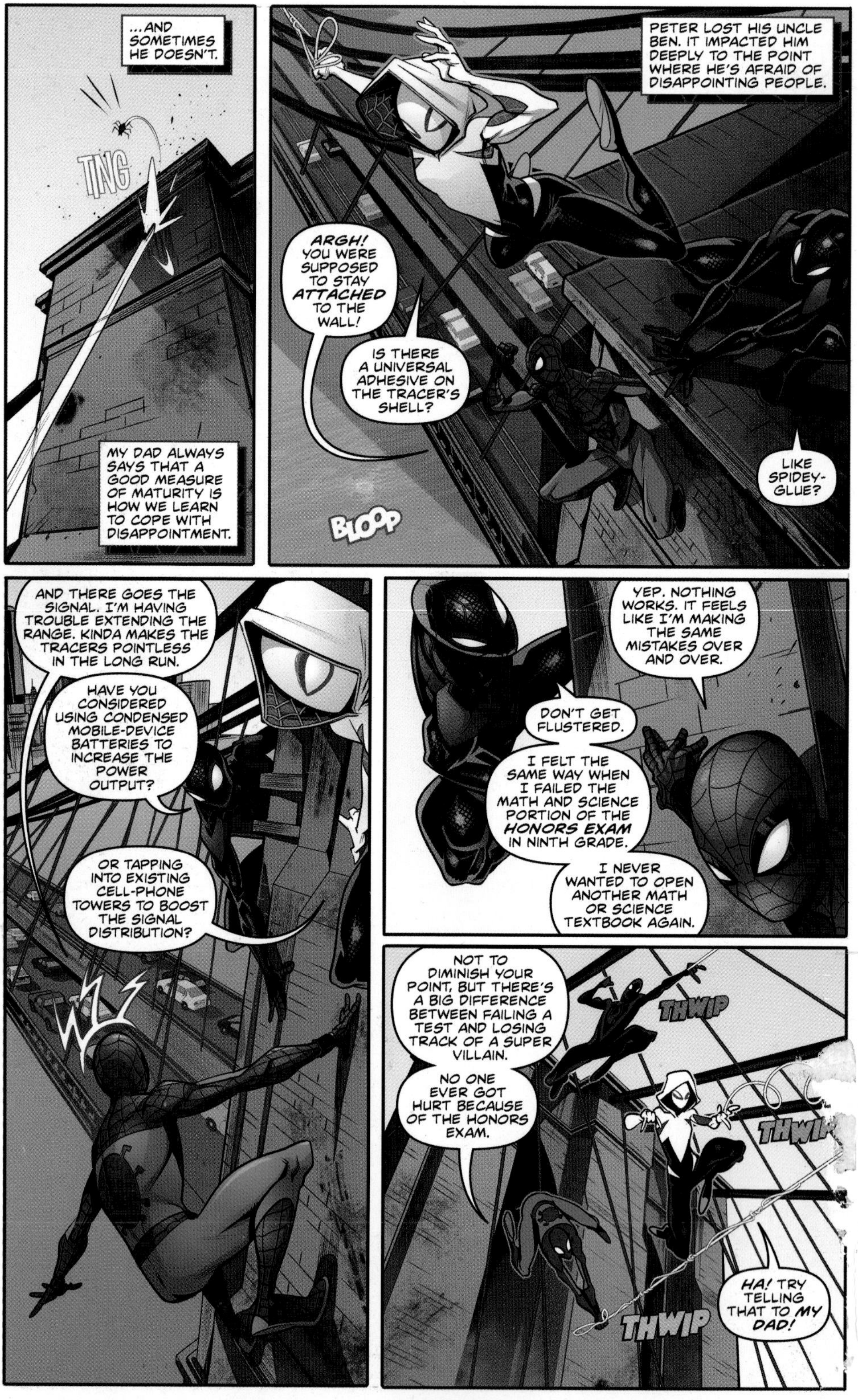
...AND SOMETIMES HE DOESN'T.
TING
MY DAD ALWAYS SAYS THAT A GOOD MEASURE OF MATURITY IS HOW WE LEARN TO COPE WITH DISAPPOINTMENT.
PETER LOST HIS UNCLE BEN. IT IMPACTED HIM DEEPLY TO THE POINT WHERE HE'S AFRAID OF DISAPPOINTING PEOPLE.
ARGH! YOU WERE SUPPOSED TO STAY ATTACHED TO THE WALL!
IS THERE A UNIVERSAL ADHESIVE ON THE TRACER'S SHELL?
LIKE SPIDEY-GLUE?
BLOOP
AND THERE GOES THE SIGNAL. I'M HAVING TROUBLE EXTENDING THE RANGE. KINDA MAKES THE TRACERS POINTLESS IN THE LONG RUN.
HAVE YOU CONSIDERED USING CONDENSED MOBILE-DEVICE BATTERIES TO INCREASE THE POWER OUTPUT?
OR TAPPING INTO EXISTING CELL-PHONE TOWERS TO BOOST THE SIGNAL DISTRIBUTION?
YEP. NOTHING WORKS. IT FEELS LIKE I'M MAKING THE SAME MISTAKES OVER AND OVER.
DON'T GET FLUSTERED.
I FELT THE SAME WAY WHEN I FAILED THE MATH AND SCIENCE PORTION OF THE HONORS EXAM IN NINTH GRADE.
I NEVER WANTED TO OPEN ANOTHER MATH OR SCIENCE TEXTBOOK AGAIN.
NOT TO DIMINISH YOUR POINT, BUT THERE'S A BIG DIFFERENCE BETWEEN FAILING A TEST AND LOSING TRACK OF A SUPER VILLAIN.
NO ONE EVER GOT HURT BECAUSE OF THE HONORS EXAM.
THWIP
THWIP
THWIP
HA! TRY TELLING THAT TO MY DAD!

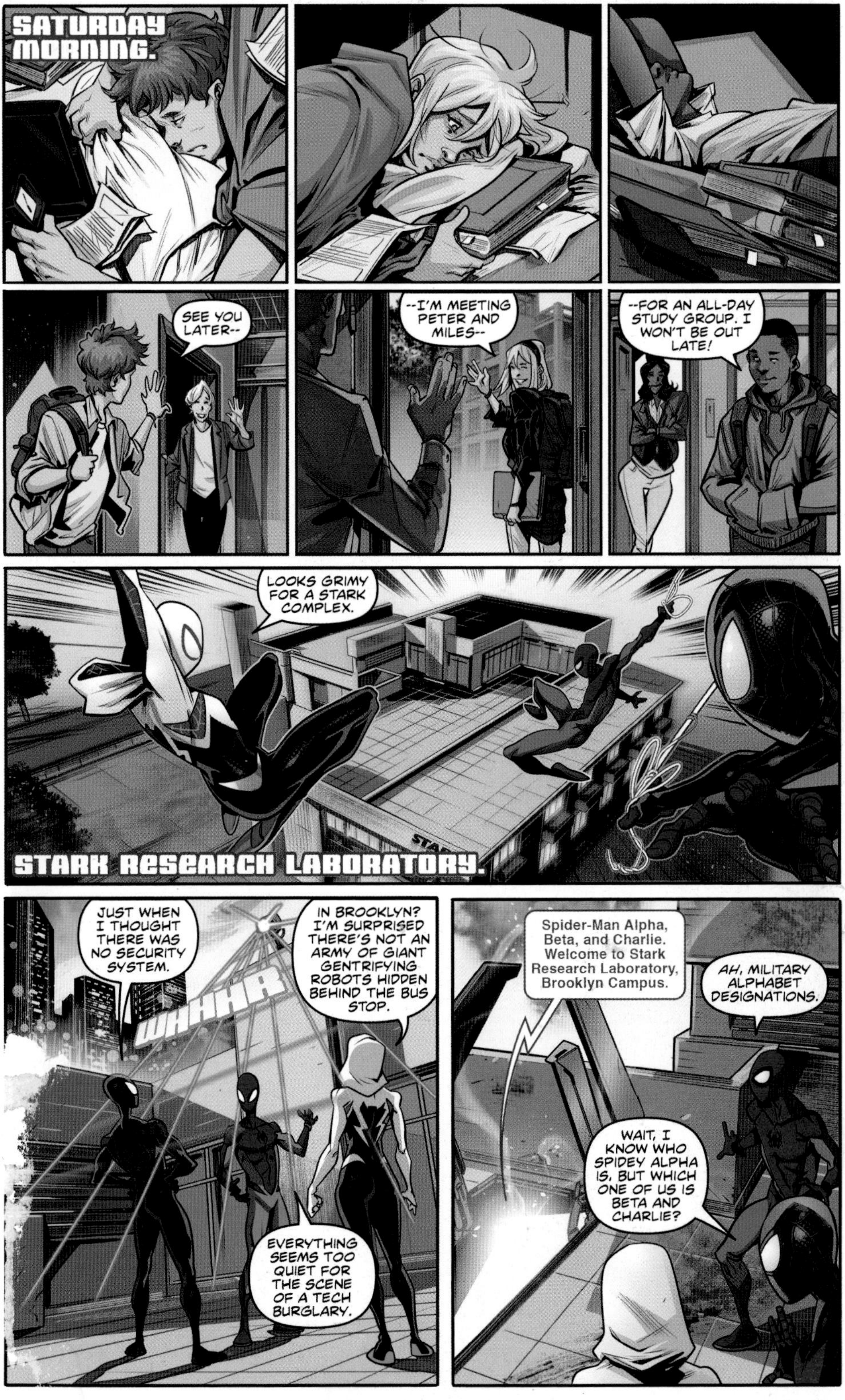
SATURDAY MORNING.
SEE YOU LATER--
--I'M MEETING PETER AND MILES--
--FOR AN ALL-DAY STUDY GROUP. I WON'T BE OUT LATE!
LOOKS GRIMY FOR A STARK COMPLEX.
STARK RESEARCH LABORATORY.
JUST WHEN I THOUGHT THERE WAS NO SECURITY SYSTEM.
IN BROOKLYN? I'M SURPRISED THERE'S NOT AN ARMY OF GIANT GENTRIFYING ROBOTS HIDDEN BEHIND THE BUS STOP.
WHHHR
EVERYTHING SEEMS TOO QUIET FOR THE SCENE OF A TECH BURGLARY.
Spider-Man Alpha, Beta, and Charlie. Welcome to Stark Research Laboratory, Brooklyn Campus.
AH, MILITARY ALPHABET DESIGNATIONS.
WAIT, I KNOW WHO SPIDEY ALPHA IS, BUT WHICH ONE OF US IS BETA AND CHARLIE?

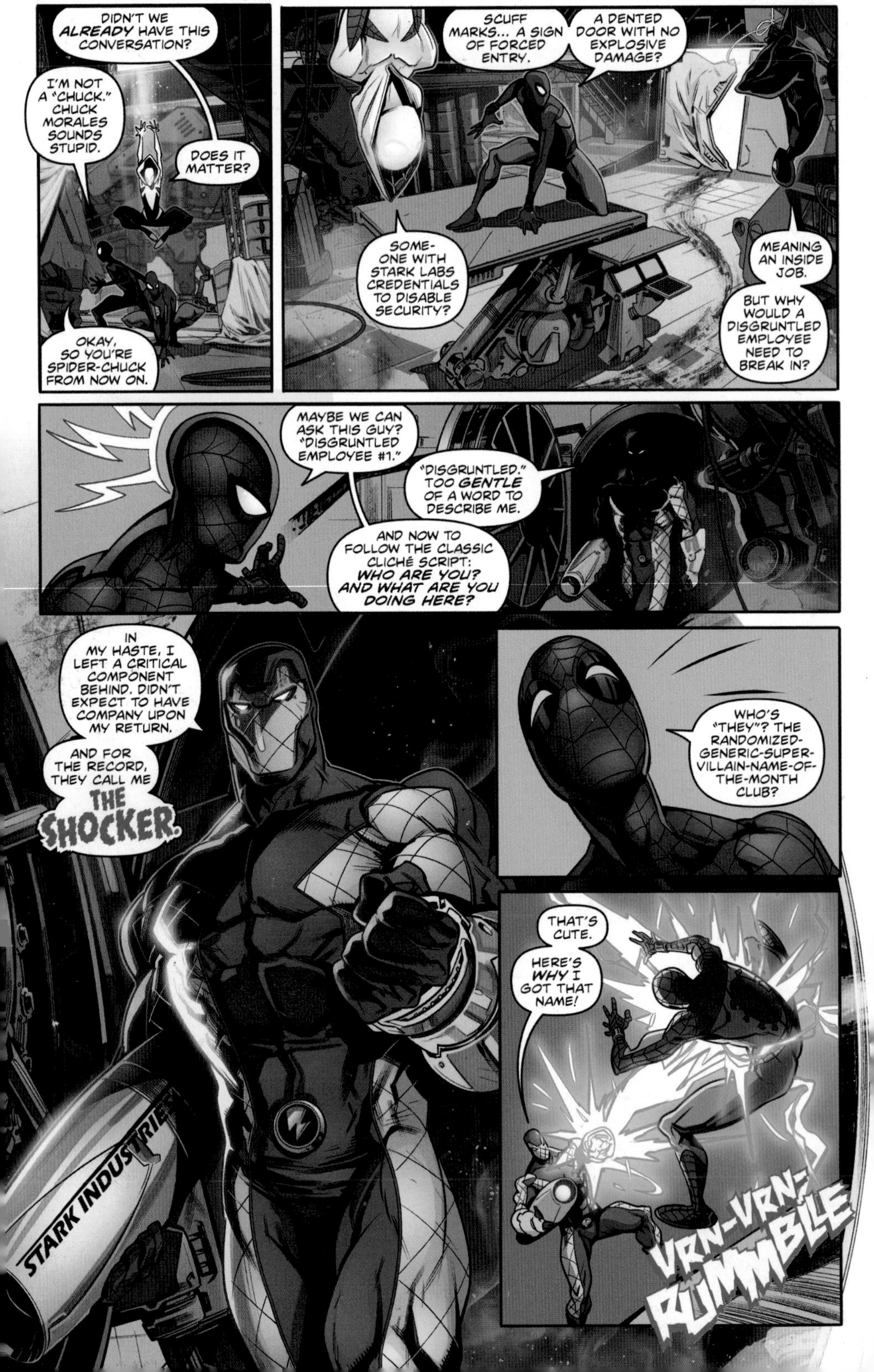
DIDN'T WE ALREADY HAVE THIS CONVERSATION?
I'M NOT A "CHUCK." CHUCK MORALES SOUNDS STUPID.
DOES IT MATTER?
OKAY, SO YOU'RE SPIDER-CHUCK FROM NOW ON.
SCUFF MARKS... A SIGN OF FORCED ENTRY.
A DENTED DOOR WITH NO EXPLOSIVE DAMAGE?
SOME-ONE WITH STARK LABS CREDENTIALS TO DISABLE SECURITY?
MEANING AN INSIDE JOB.
BUT WHY WOULD A DISGRUNTLED EMPLOYEE NEED TO BREAK IN?
MAYBE WE CAN ASK THIS GUY? "DISGRUNTLED EMPLOYEE #1."
"DISGRUNTLED." TOO GENTLE OF A WORD TO DESCRIBE ME.
AND NOW TO FOLLOW THE CLASSIC CLICHÉ SCRIPT: WHO ARE YOU? AND WHAT ARE YOU DOING HERE?
IN MY HASTE, I LEFT A CRITICAL COMPONENT BEHIND. DIDN'T EXPECT TO HAVE COMPANY UPON MY RETURN.
AND FOR THE RECORD, THEY CALL ME
THE SHOCKER.
STARK INDUSTRIES
WHO'S "THEY"? THE RANDOMIZED-GENERIC-SUPER-VILLAIN-NAME-OF-THE-MONTH CLUB?
THAT'S CUTE.
HERE'S WHY I GOT THAT NAME!
VRN-VRN-RUMMBLLE

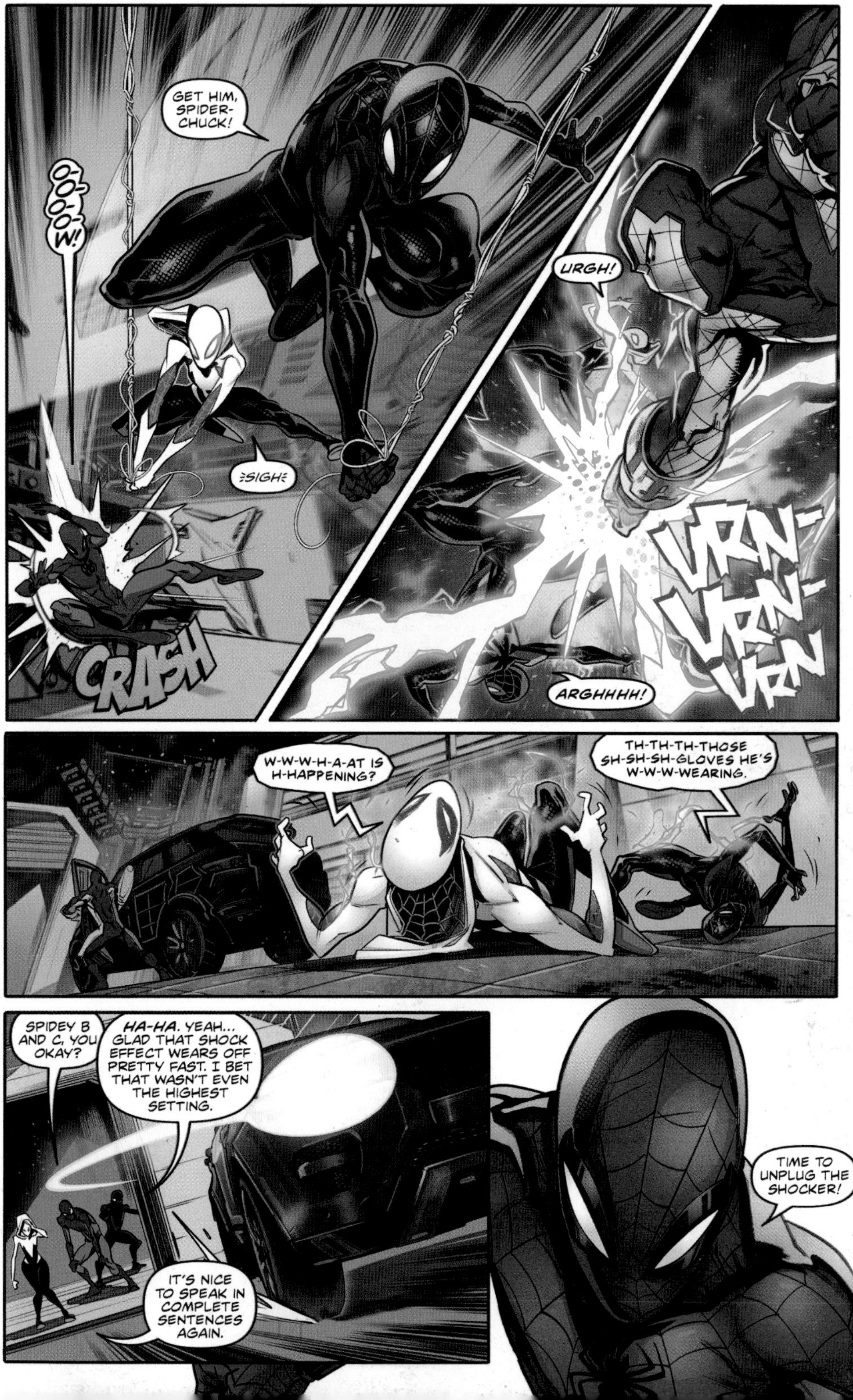
GET HIM, SPIDER-CHUCK!
O-O-O-O-OW!
≈SIGH≈
CRASH
URGH!
ARGHHHH!
VRN-VRN-VRN
W-W-W-H-A-AT IS H-HAPPENING?
TH-TH-TH-THOSE SH-SH-SH-GLOVES HE'S W-W-W-WEARING.
SPIDEY B AND C, YOU OKAY?
HA-HA. YEAH... GLAD THAT SHOCK EFFECT WEARS OFF PRETTY FAST. I BET THAT WASN'T EVEN THE HIGHEST SETTING.
IT'S NICE TO SPEAK IN COMPLETE SENTENCES AGAIN.
TIME TO UNPLUG THE SHOCKER!

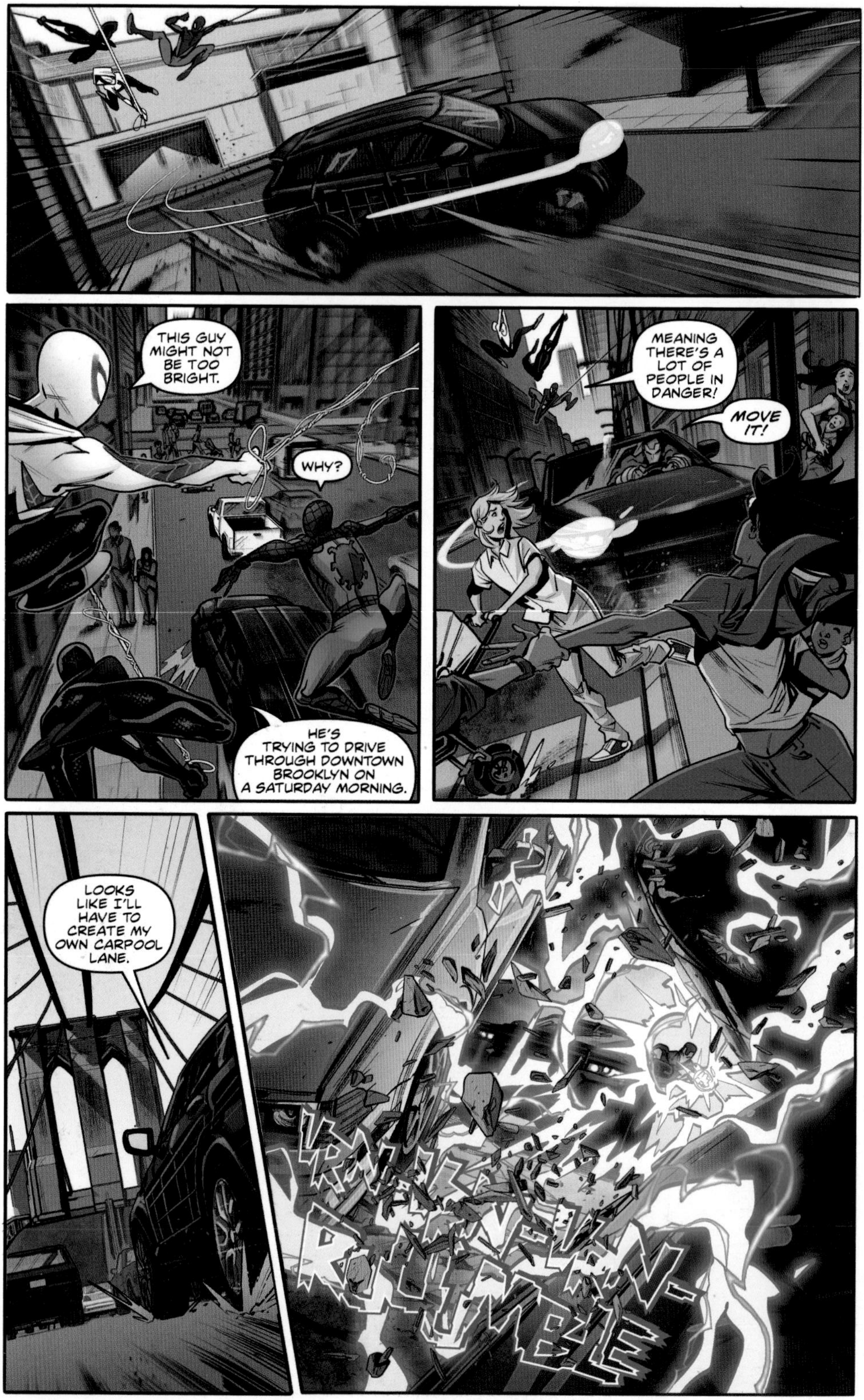
THIS GUY MIGHT NOT BE TOO BRIGHT.
WHY?
HE'S TRYING TO DRIVE THROUGH DOWNTOWN BROOKLYN ON A SATURDAY MORNING.
MEANING THERE'S A LOT OF PEOPLE IN DANGER!
MOVE IT!
LOOKS LIKE I'LL HAVE TO CREATE MY OWN CARPOOL LANE.

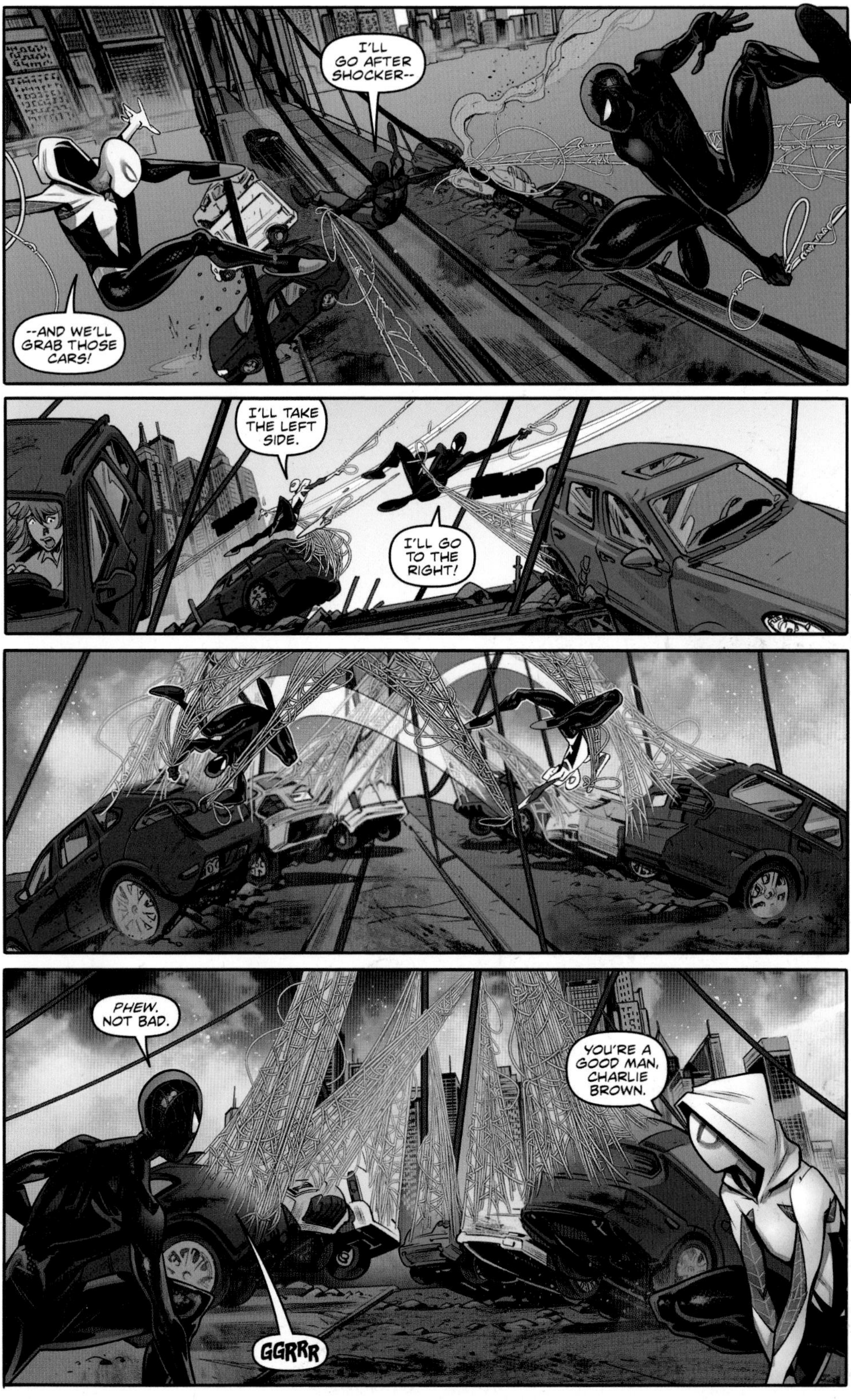
I'LL GO AFTER SHOCKER--
--AND WE'LL GRAB THOSE CARS!
I'LL TAKE THE LEFT SIDE.
I'LL GO TO THE RIGHT!
*PHEW.* NOT BAD.
YOU'RE A GOOD MAN, CHARLIE BROWN.
GGRRR

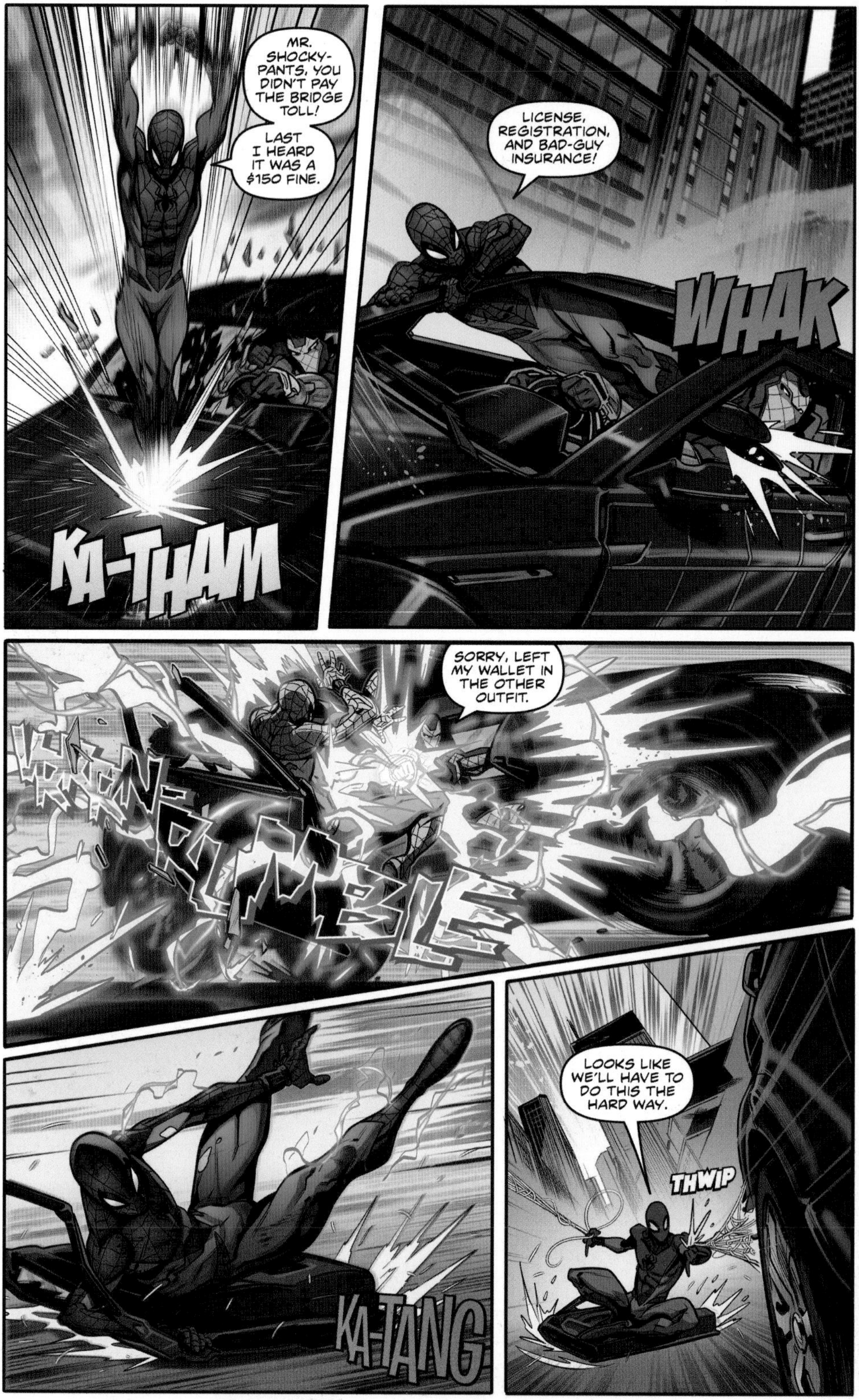
MR. SHOCKY-PANTS, YOU DIDN'T PAY THE BRIDGE TOLL!
LAST I HEARD IT WAS A $150 FINE.
KA-THAM
LICENSE, REGISTRATION, AND BAD-GUY INSURANCE!
WHAK
SORRY, LEFT MY WALLET IN THE OTHER OUTFIT.
KA-TANG
LOOKS LIKE WE'LL HAVE TO DO THIS THE HARD WAY.
THWIP

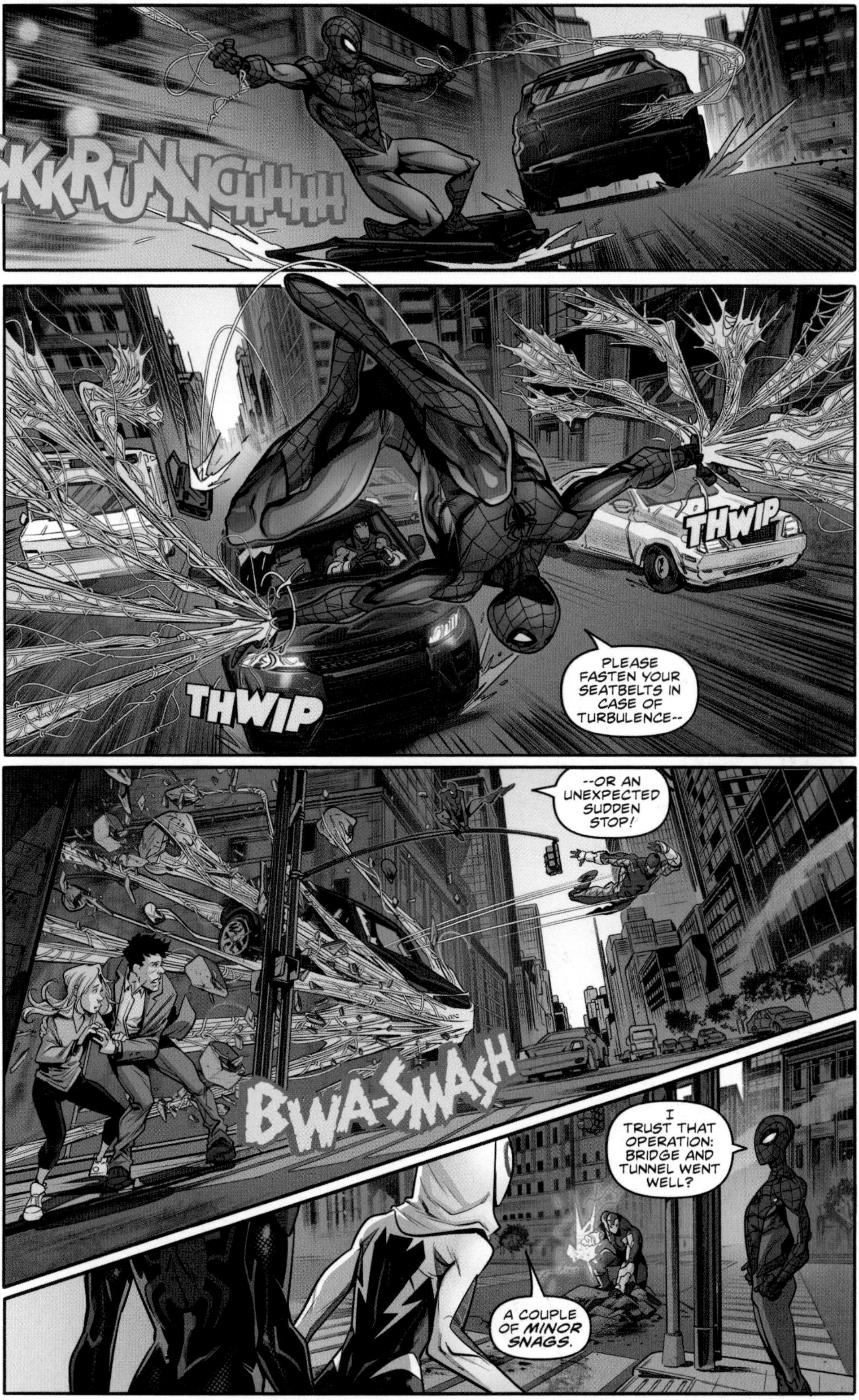
SKKRUNNCHHHH
PLEASE FASTEN YOUR SEATBELTS IN CASE OF TURBULENCE--
THWIP
THWIP
--OR AN UNEXPECTED SUDDEN STOP!
BWA-SMASH
I TRUST THAT OPERATION: BRIDGE AND TUNNEL WENT WELL?
A COUPLE OF MINOR SNAGS.

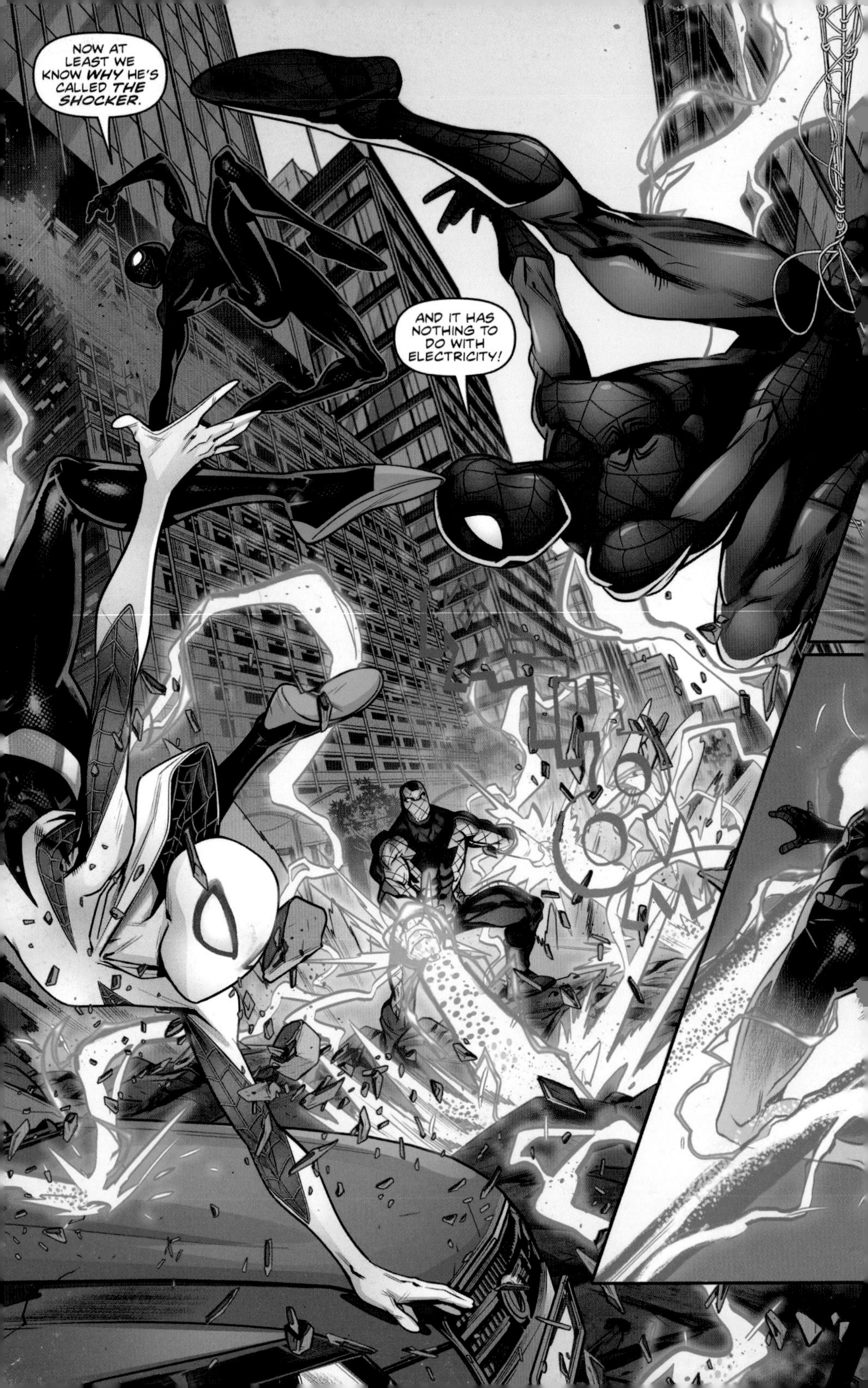
NOW AT LEAST WE KNOW WHY HE'S CALLED THE SHOCKER.
AND IT HAS NOTHING TO DO WITH ELECTRICITY!

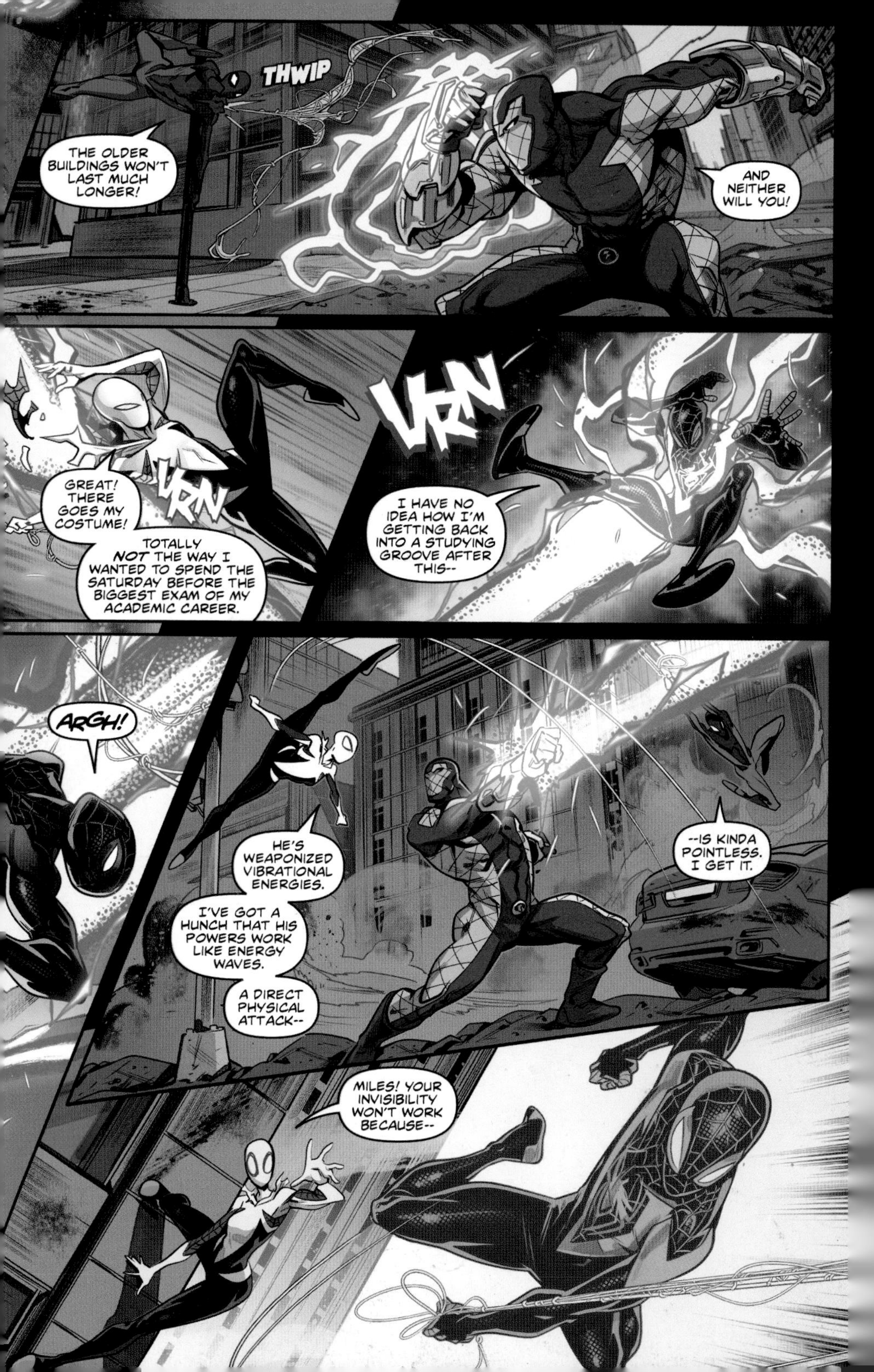
THWIP
THE OLDER BUILDINGS WON'T LAST MUCH LONGER!
AND NEITHER WILL YOU!
GREAT! THERE GOES MY COSTUME!
VRN
TOTALLY *NOT* THE WAY I WANTED TO SPEND THE SATURDAY BEFORE THE BIGGEST EXAM OF MY ACADEMIC CAREER.
VRN
I HAVE NO IDEA HOW I'M GETTING BACK INTO A STUDYING GROOVE AFTER THIS--
ARGH!
HE'S WEAPONIZED VIBRATIONAL ENERGIES.
I'VE GOT A HUNCH THAT HIS POWERS WORK LIKE ENERGY WAVES.
A DIRECT PHYSICAL ATTACK--
--IS KINDA POINTLESS. I GET IT.
MILES! YOUR INVISIBILITY WON'T WORK BECAUSE--

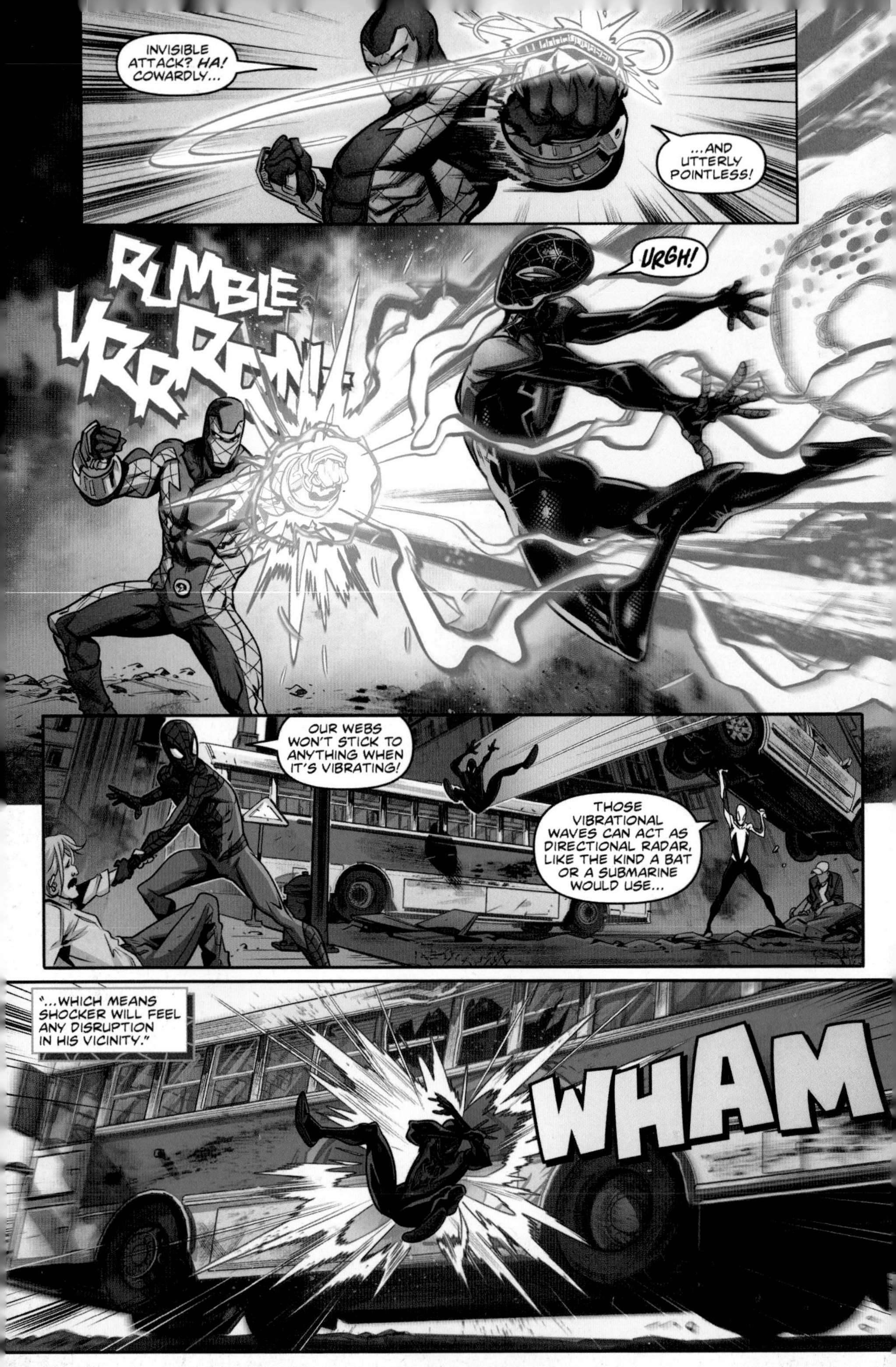
INVISIBLE ATTACK? HA! COWARDLY...
...AND UTTERLY POINTLESS!
RUMBLE
URGH!
VRRRONN
OUR WEBS WON'T STICK TO ANYTHING WHEN IT'S VIBRATING!
THOSE VIBRATIONAL WAVES CAN ACT AS DIRECTIONAL RADAR, LIKE THE KIND A BAT OR A SUBMARINE WOULD USE...
"...WHICH MEANS SHOCKER WILL FEEL ANY DISRUPTION IN HIS VICINITY."
WHAM

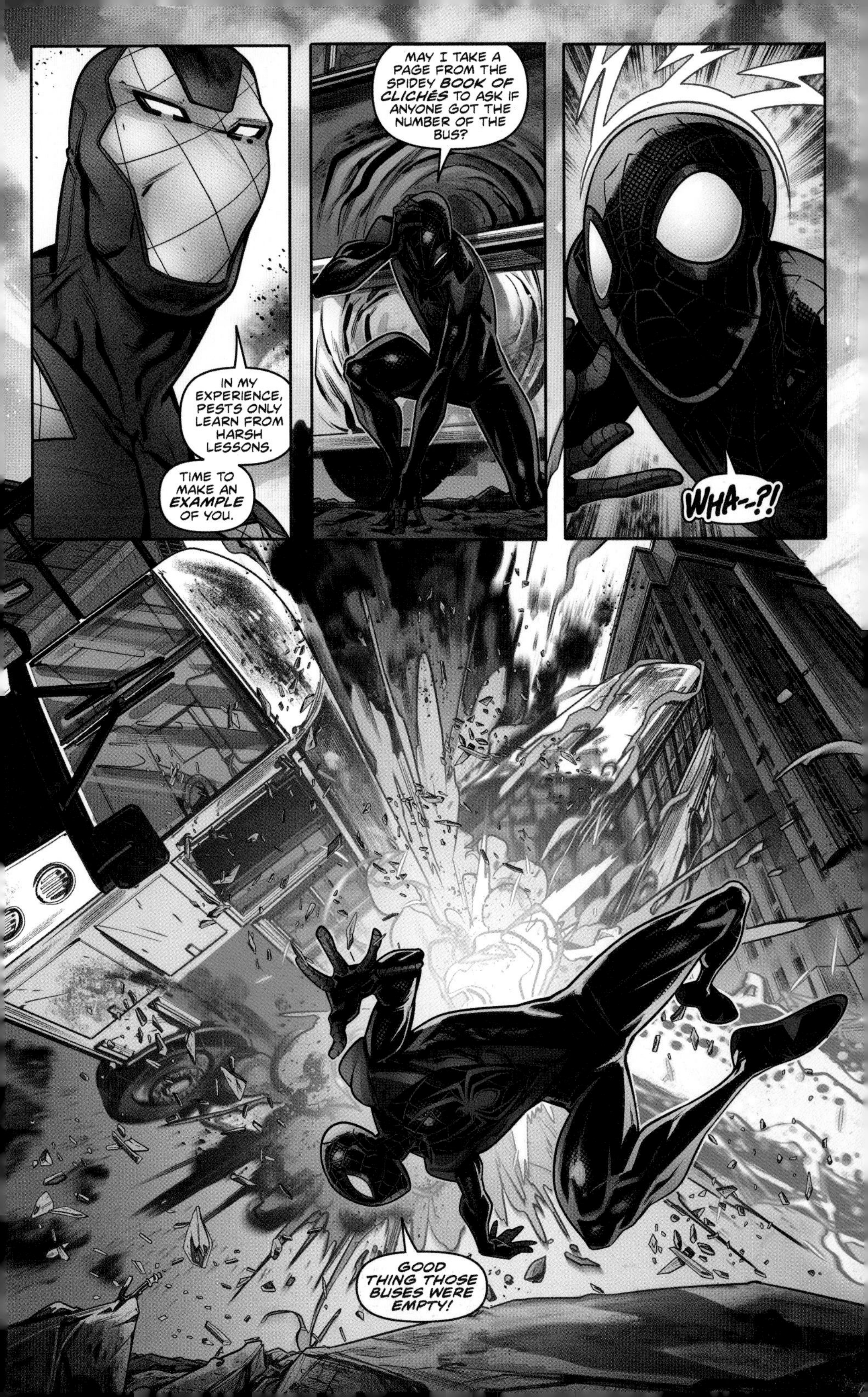
IN MY EXPERIENCE, PESTS ONLY LEARN FROM HARSH LESSONS.
TIME TO MAKE AN *EXAMPLE* OF YOU.
MAY I TAKE A PAGE FROM THE SPIDEY *BOOK OF CLICHÉS* TO ASK IF ANYONE GOT THE NUMBER OF THE BUS?
WHA--?!
GOOD THING THOSE BUSES WERE EMPTY!

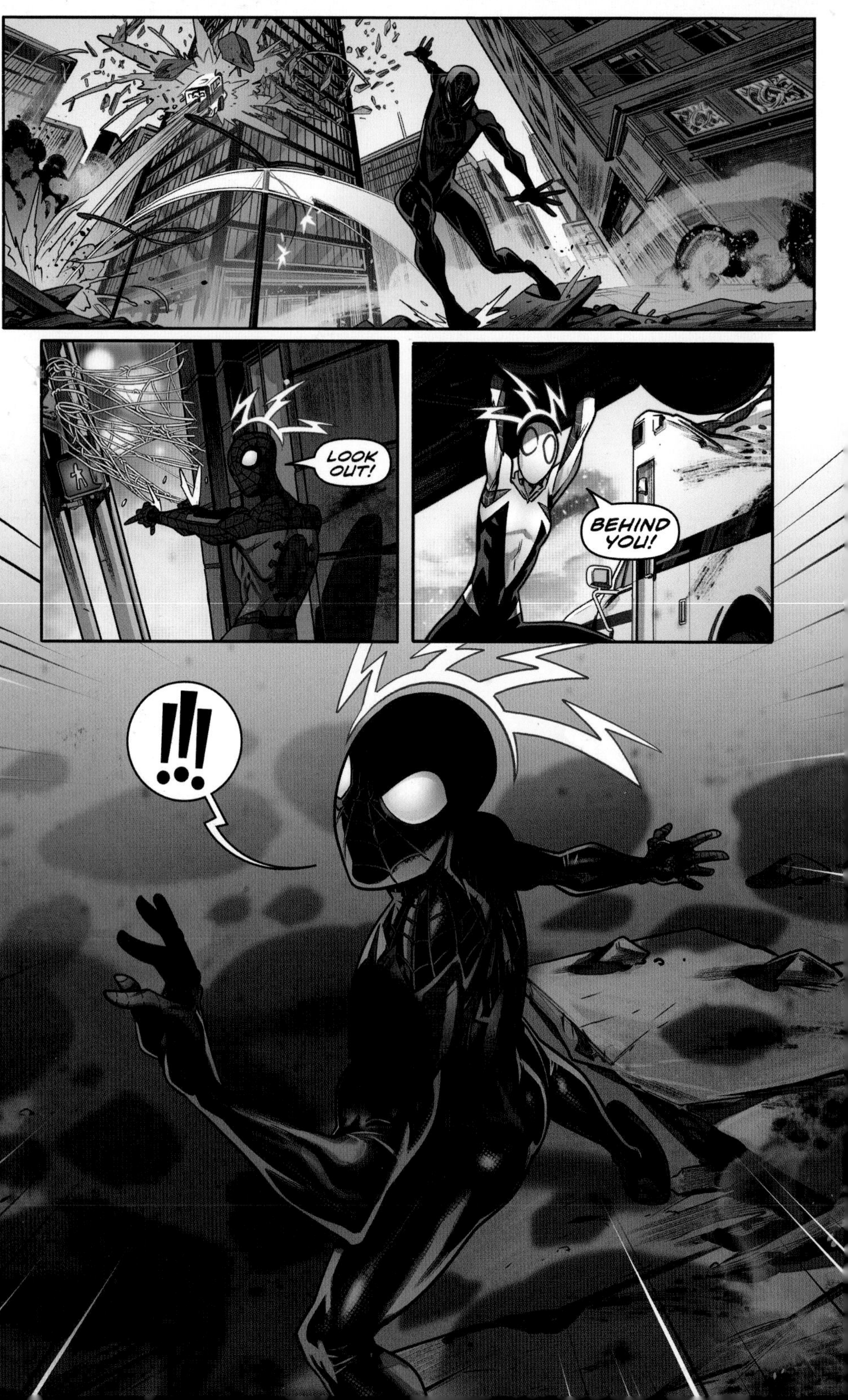
LOOK OUT!
BEHIND YOU!
!!!

# PART TWO

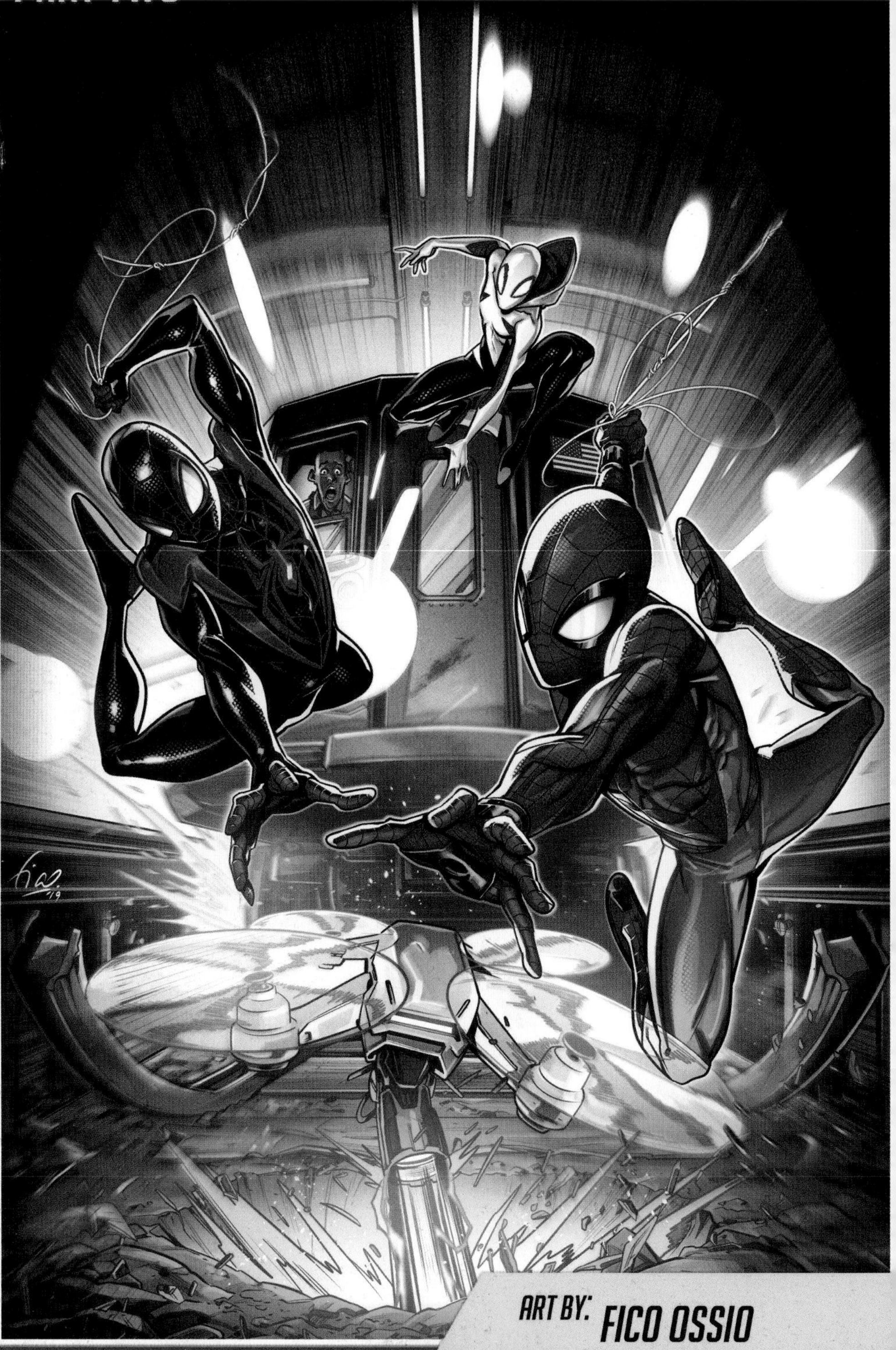

ART BY: FICO OSSIO

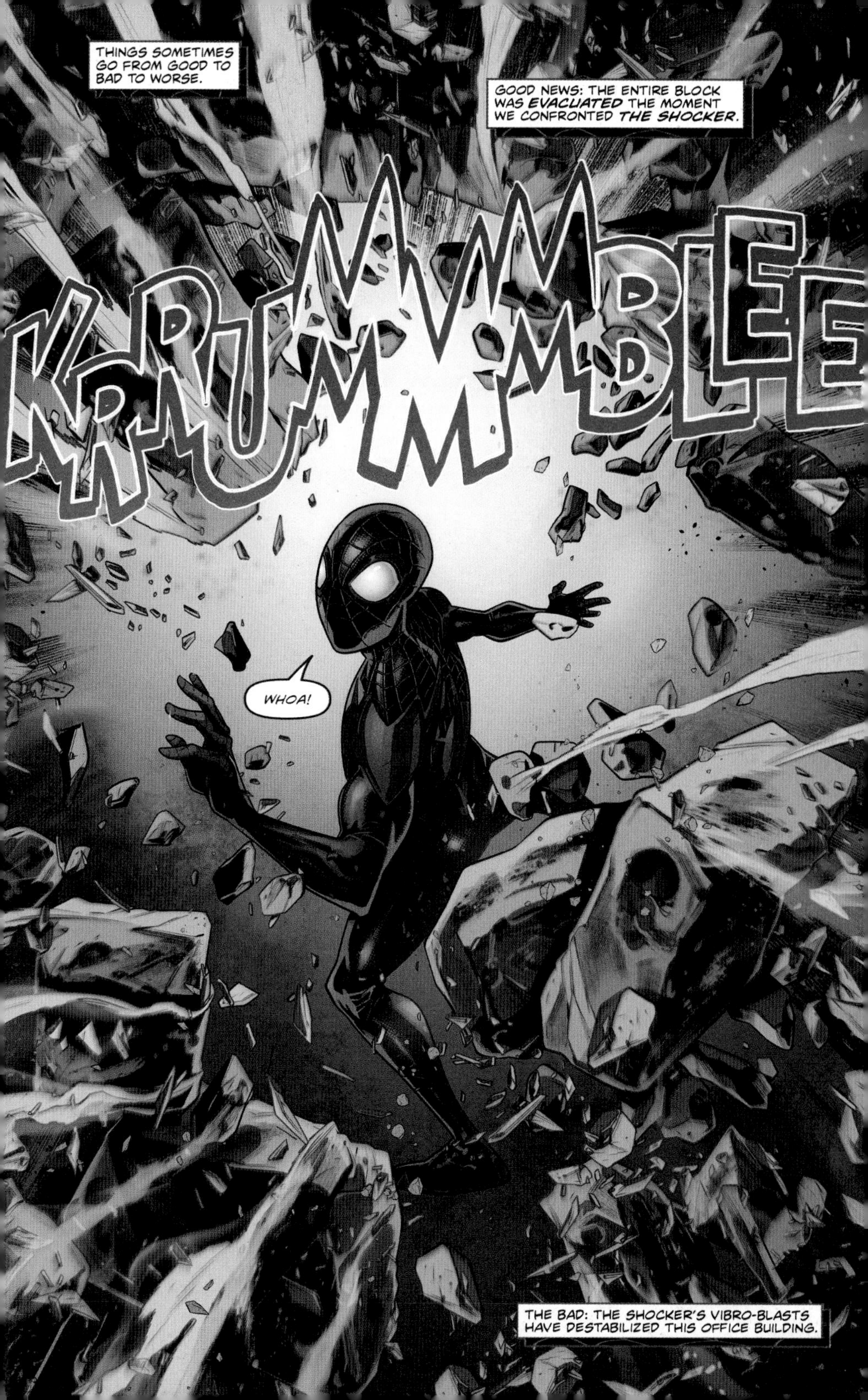
THINGS SOMETIMES GO FROM GOOD TO BAD TO WORSE.
GOOD NEWS: THE ENTIRE BLOCK WAS EVACUATED THE MOMENT WE CONFRONTED THE SHOCKER.
KRRUMMMBLEE
WHOA!
THE BAD: THE SHOCKER'S VIBRO-BLASTS HAVE DESTABILIZED THIS OFFICE BUILDING.

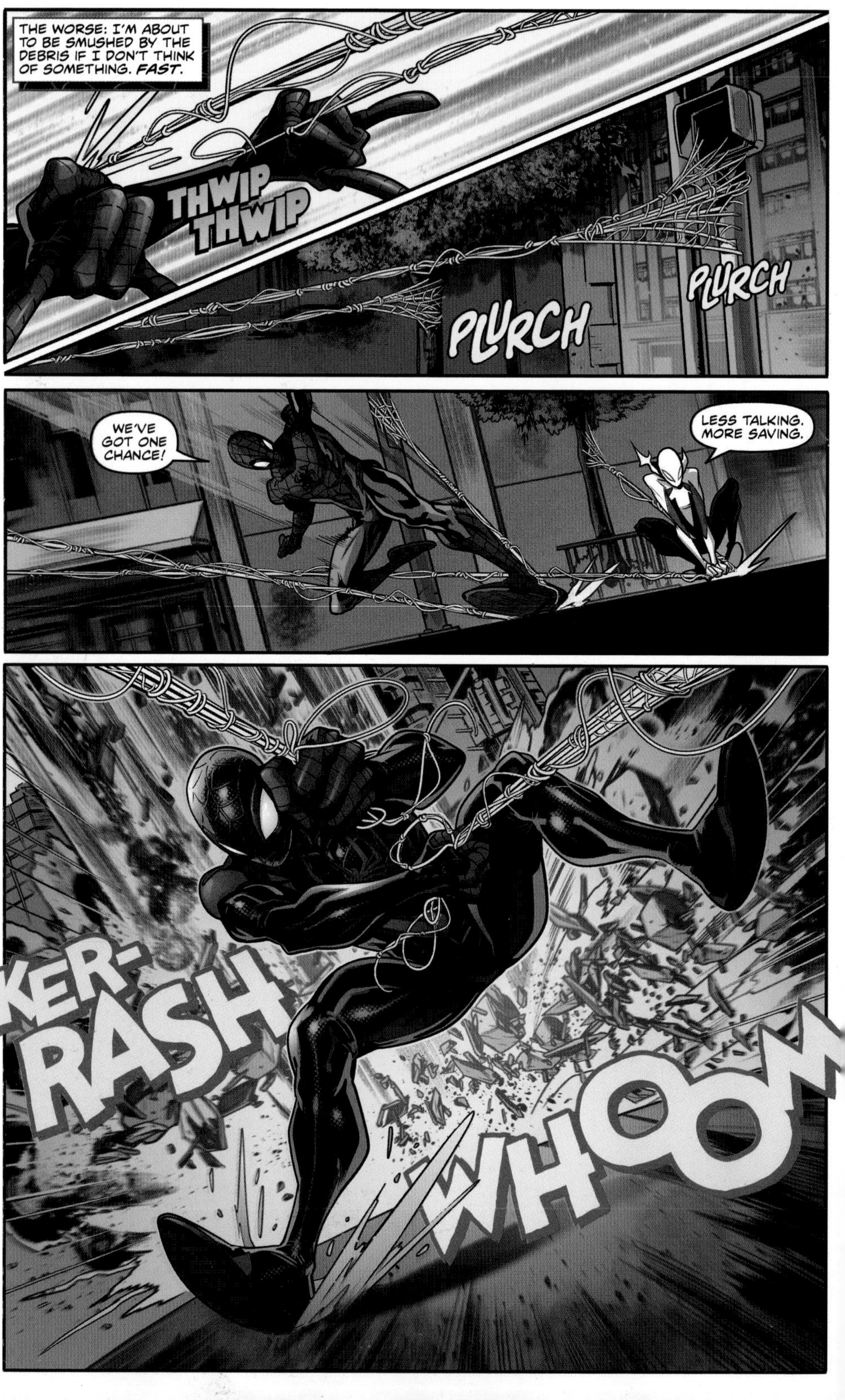
THE WORSE: I'M ABOUT TO BE SMUSHED BY THE DEBRIS IF I DON'T THINK OF SOMETHING. FAST.
THWIP THWIP
PLURCH
PLURCH
WE'VE GOT ONE CHANCE!
LESS TALKING. MORE SAVING.
KER-RASH
WHOOM

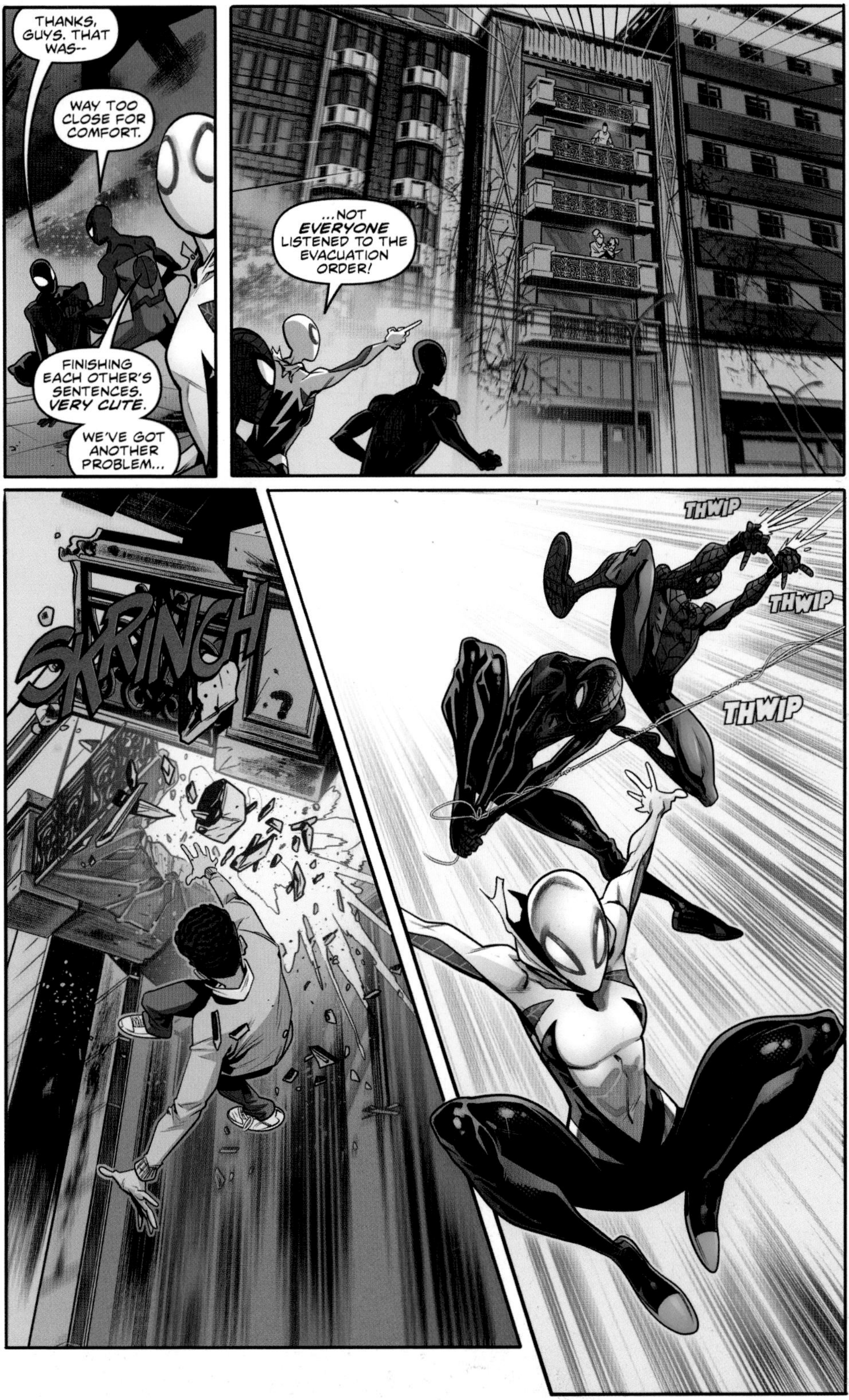
THANKS, GUYS. THAT WAS--
WAY TOO CLOSE FOR COMFORT.
FINISHING EACH OTHER'S SENTENCES. VERY CUTE.
WE'VE GOT ANOTHER PROBLEM...
...NOT EVERYONE LISTENED TO THE EVACUATION ORDER!
SKRINCH
THWIP
THWIP
THWIP

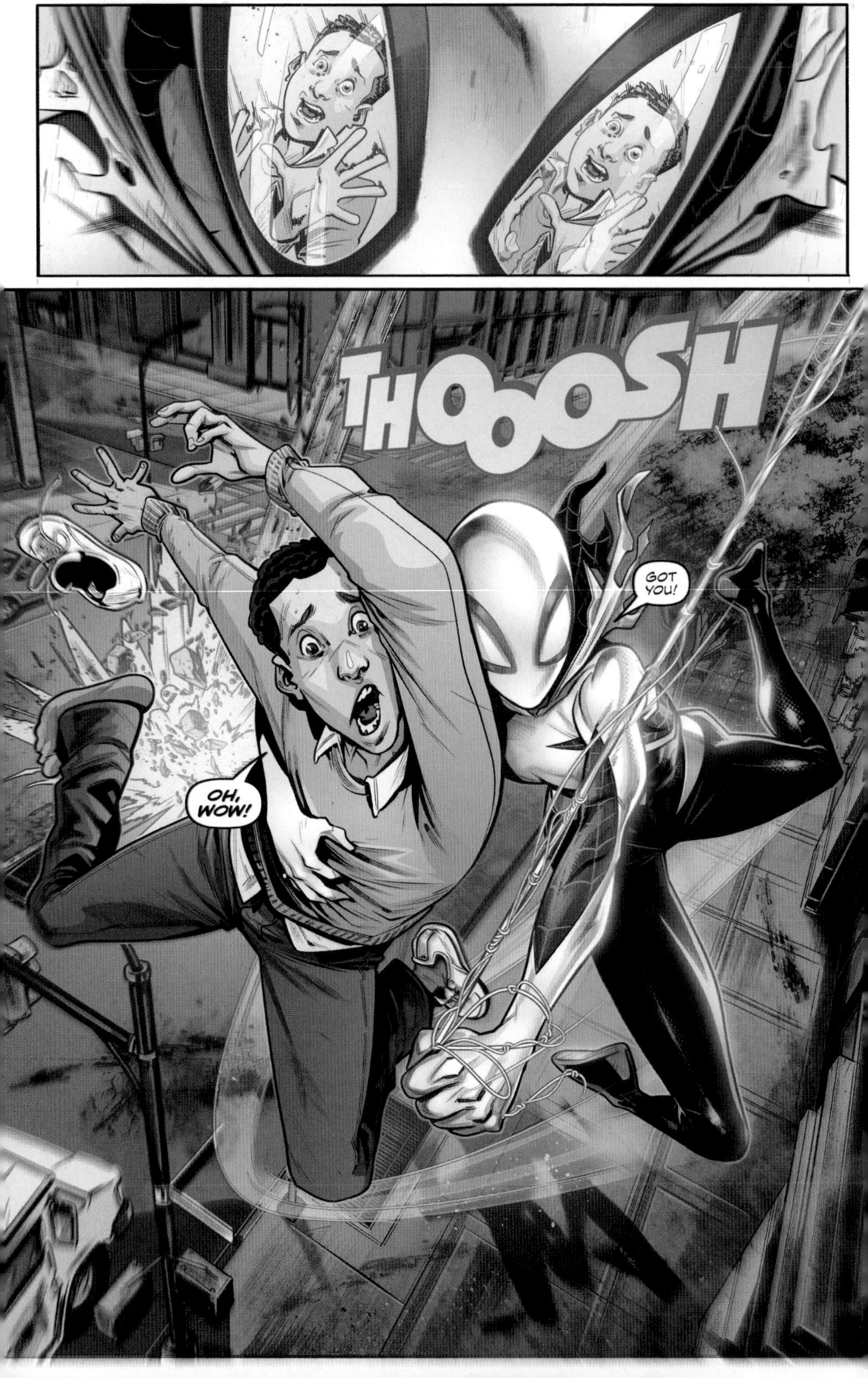
THOOOSH
GOT YOU!
OH, WOW!

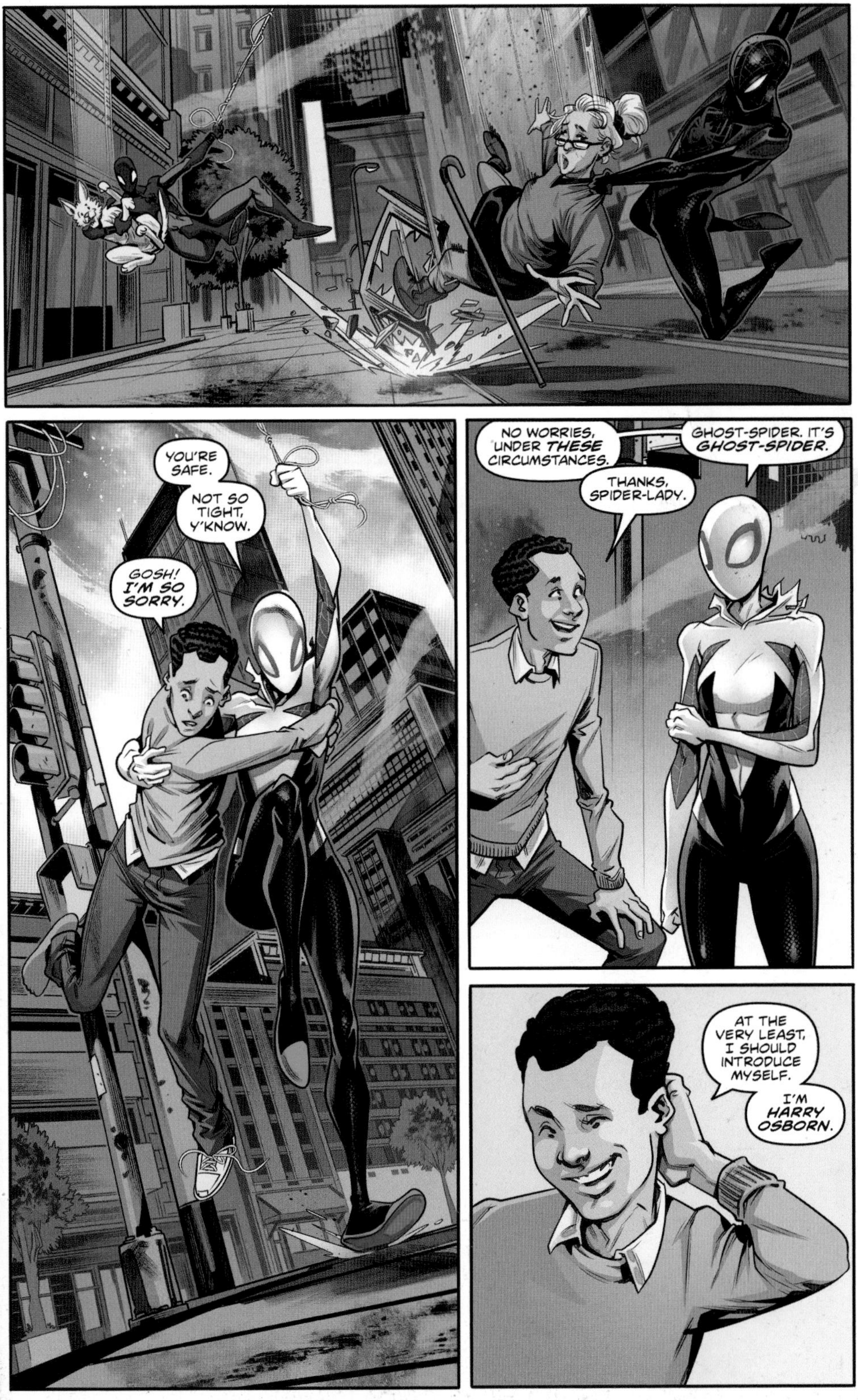

YOU'RE SAFE.
NOT SO TIGHT, Y'KNOW.
GOSH! I'M SO SORRY.
NO WORRIES, UNDER THESE CIRCUMSTANCES.
THANKS, SPIDER-LADY.
GHOST-SPIDER. IT'S GHOST-SPIDER.
AT THE VERY LEAST, I SHOULD INTRODUCE MYSELF.
I'M HARRY OSBORN.

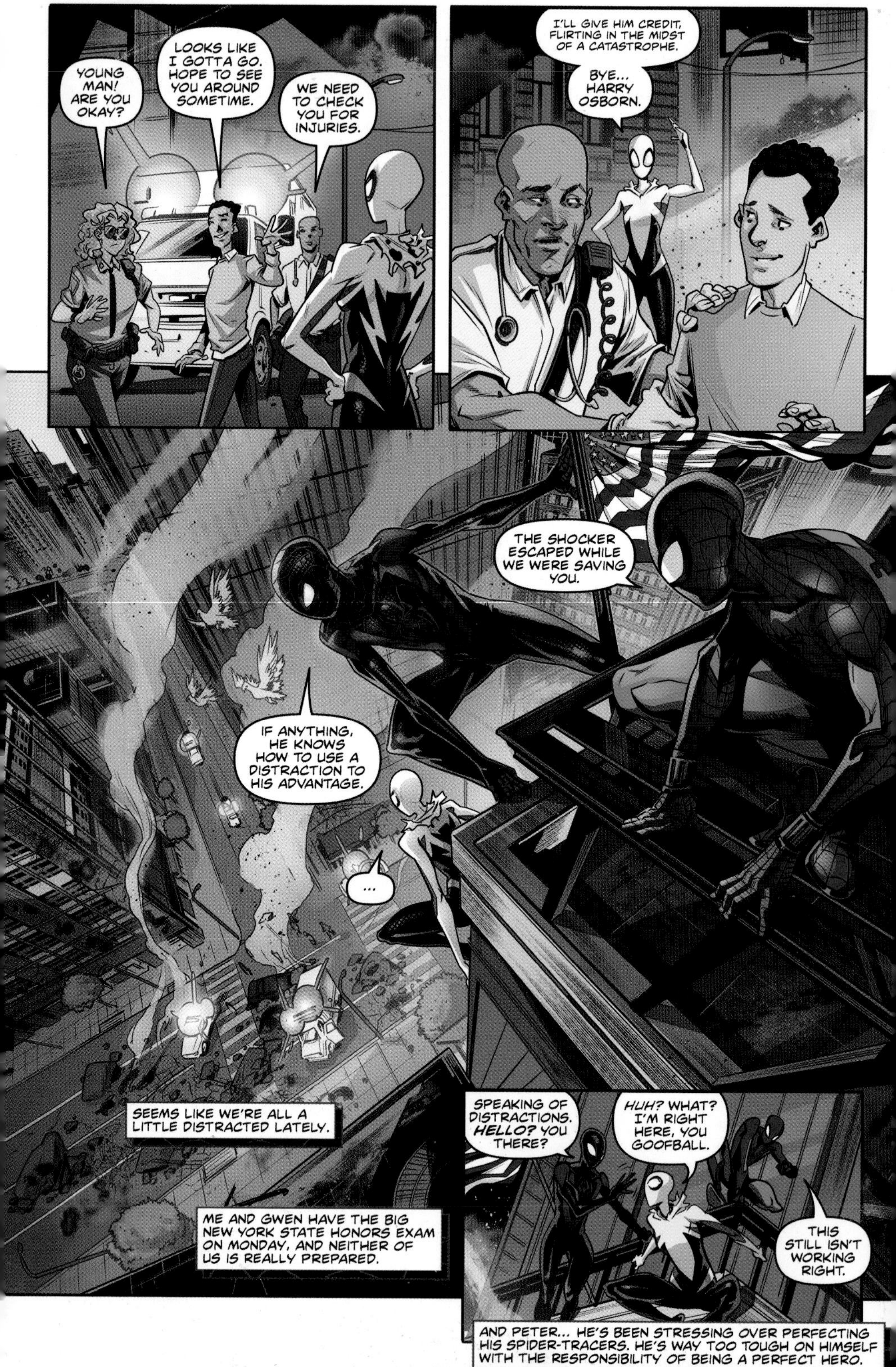
YOUNG MAN! ARE YOU OKAY?
LOOKS LIKE I GOTTA GO. HOPE TO SEE YOU AROUND SOMETIME.
WE NEED TO CHECK YOU FOR INJURIES.
I'LL GIVE HIM CREDIT, FLIRTING IN THE MIDST OF A CATASTROPHE.
BYE... HARRY OSBORN.
THE SHOCKER ESCAPED WHILE WE WERE SAVING YOU.
IF ANYTHING, HE KNOWS HOW TO USE A DISTRACTION TO HIS ADVANTAGE.
...
SEEMS LIKE WE'RE ALL A LITTLE DISTRACTED LATELY.
ME AND GWEN HAVE THE BIG NEW YORK STATE HONORS EXAM ON MONDAY, AND NEITHER OF US IS REALLY PREPARED.
SPEAKING OF DISTRACTIONS. *HELLO?* YOU THERE?
*HUH?* WHAT? I'M RIGHT HERE, YOU GOOFBALL.
THIS STILL ISN'T WORKING RIGHT.
AND PETER... HE'S BEEN STRESSING OVER PERFECTING HIS SPIDER-TRACERS. HE'S WAY TOO TOUGH ON HIMSELF WITH THE RESPONSIBILITY OF BEING A PERFECT HERO.

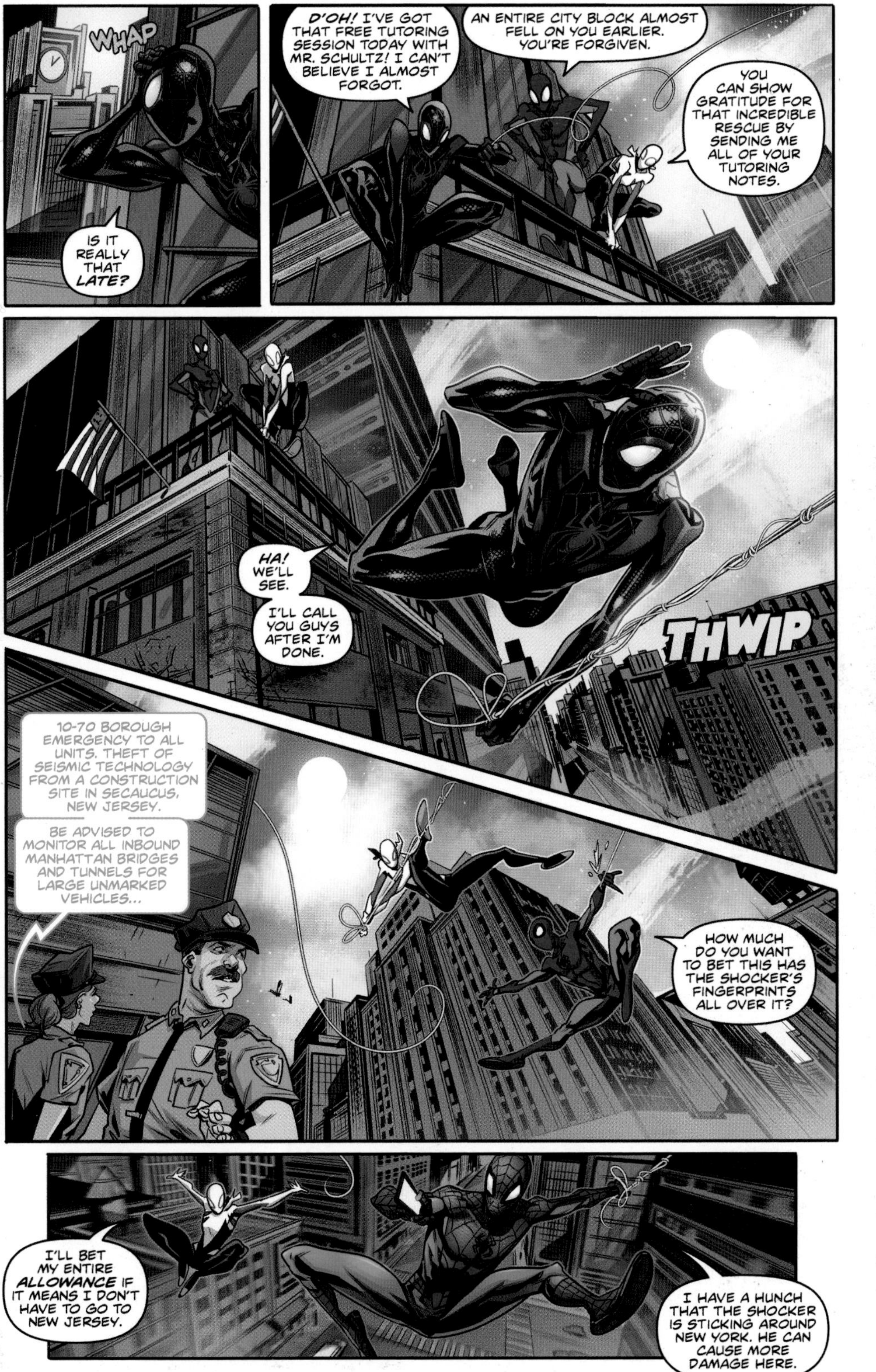
WHAP
IS IT REALLY THAT LATE?
D'OH! I'VE GOT THAT FREE TUTORING SESSION TODAY WITH MR. SCHULTZ! I CAN'T BELIEVE I ALMOST FORGOT.
AN ENTIRE CITY BLOCK ALMOST FELL ON YOU EARLIER. YOU'RE FORGIVEN.
YOU CAN SHOW GRATITUDE FOR THAT INCREDIBLE RESCUE BY SENDING ME ALL OF YOUR TUTORING NOTES.
HA! WE'LL SEE.
I'LL CALL YOU GUYS AFTER I'M DONE.
THWIP
10-70 BOROUGH EMERGENCY TO ALL UNITS. THEFT OF SEISMIC TECHNOLOGY FROM A CONSTRUCTION SITE IN SECAUCUS, NEW JERSEY.
BE ADVISED TO MONITOR ALL INBOUND MANHATTAN BRIDGES AND TUNNELS FOR LARGE UNMARKED VEHICLES...
HOW MUCH DO YOU WANT TO BET THIS HAS THE SHOCKER'S FINGERPRINTS ALL OVER IT?
I'LL BET MY ENTIRE ALLOWANCE IF IT MEANS I DON'T HAVE TO GO TO NEW JERSEY.
I HAVE A HUNCH THAT THE SHOCKER IS STICKING AROUND NEW YORK. HE CAN CAUSE MORE DAMAGE HERE.

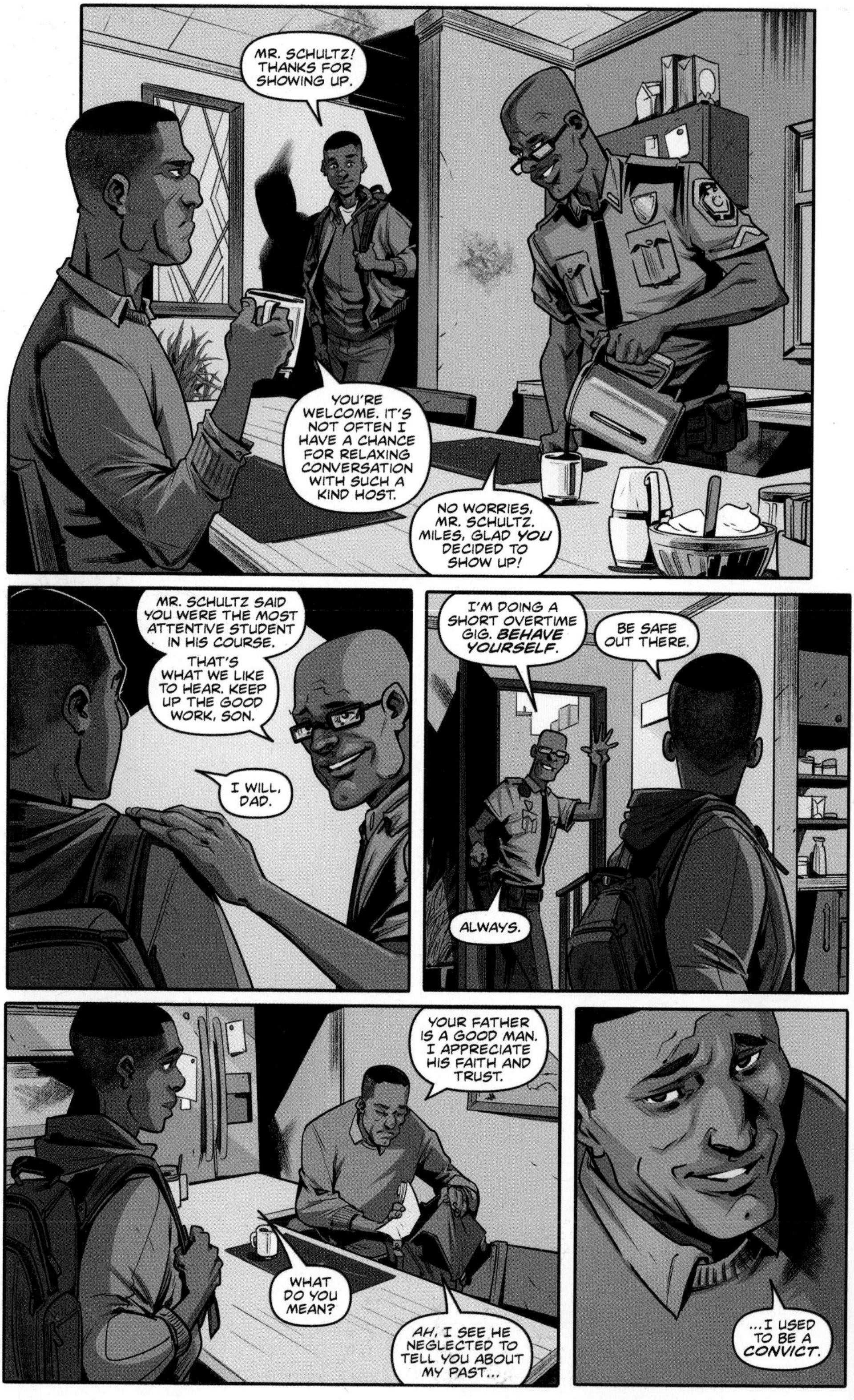
MR. SCHULTZ! THANKS FOR SHOWING UP.
YOU'RE WELCOME. IT'S NOT OFTEN I HAVE A CHANCE FOR RELAXING CONVERSATION WITH SUCH A KIND HOST.
NO WORRIES, MR. SCHULTZ. MILES, GLAD YOU DECIDED TO SHOW UP!
MR. SCHULTZ SAID YOU WERE THE MOST ATTENTIVE STUDENT IN HIS COURSE.
THAT'S WHAT WE LIKE TO HEAR. KEEP UP THE GOOD WORK, SON.
I WILL, DAD.
I'M DOING A SHORT OVERTIME GIG. BEHAVE YOURSELF.
BE SAFE OUT THERE.
ALWAYS.
YOUR FATHER IS A GOOD MAN. I APPRECIATE HIS FAITH AND TRUST.
WHAT DO YOU MEAN?
AH, I SEE HE NEGLECTED TO TELL YOU ABOUT MY PAST...
...I USED TO BE A CONVICT.

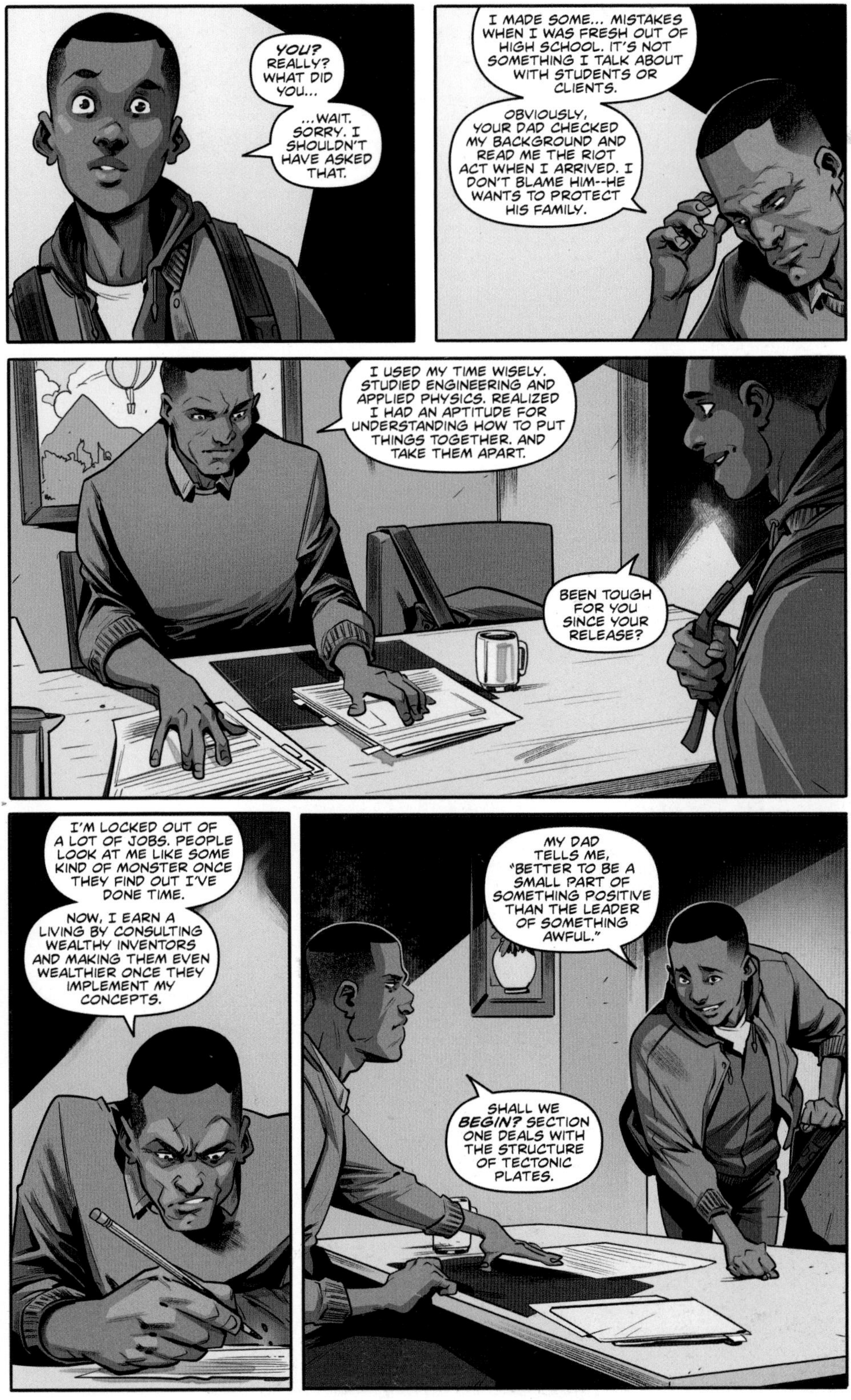
YOU? REALLY? WHAT DID YOU...
...WAIT. SORRY. I SHOULDN'T HAVE ASKED THAT.
I MADE SOME... MISTAKES WHEN I WAS FRESH OUT OF HIGH SCHOOL. IT'S NOT SOMETHING I TALK ABOUT WITH STUDENTS OR CLIENTS.
OBVIOUSLY, YOUR DAD CHECKED MY BACKGROUND AND READ ME THE RIOT ACT WHEN I ARRIVED. I DON'T BLAME HIM--HE WANTS TO PROTECT HIS FAMILY.
I USED MY TIME WISELY. STUDIED ENGINEERING AND APPLIED PHYSICS. REALIZED I HAD AN APTITUDE FOR UNDERSTANDING HOW TO PUT THINGS TOGETHER. AND TAKE THEM APART.
BEEN TOUGH FOR YOU SINCE YOUR RELEASE?
I'M LOCKED OUT OF A LOT OF JOBS. PEOPLE LOOK AT ME LIKE SOME KIND OF MONSTER ONCE THEY FIND OUT I'VE DONE TIME.
NOW, I EARN A LIVING BY CONSULTING WEALTHY INVENTORS AND MAKING THEM EVEN WEALTHIER ONCE THEY IMPLEMENT MY CONCEPTS.
MY DAD TELLS ME, "BETTER TO BE A SMALL PART OF SOMETHING POSITIVE THAN THE LEADER OF SOMETHING AWFUL."
SHALL WE BEGIN? SECTION ONE DEALS WITH THE STRUCTURE OF TECTONIC PLATES.

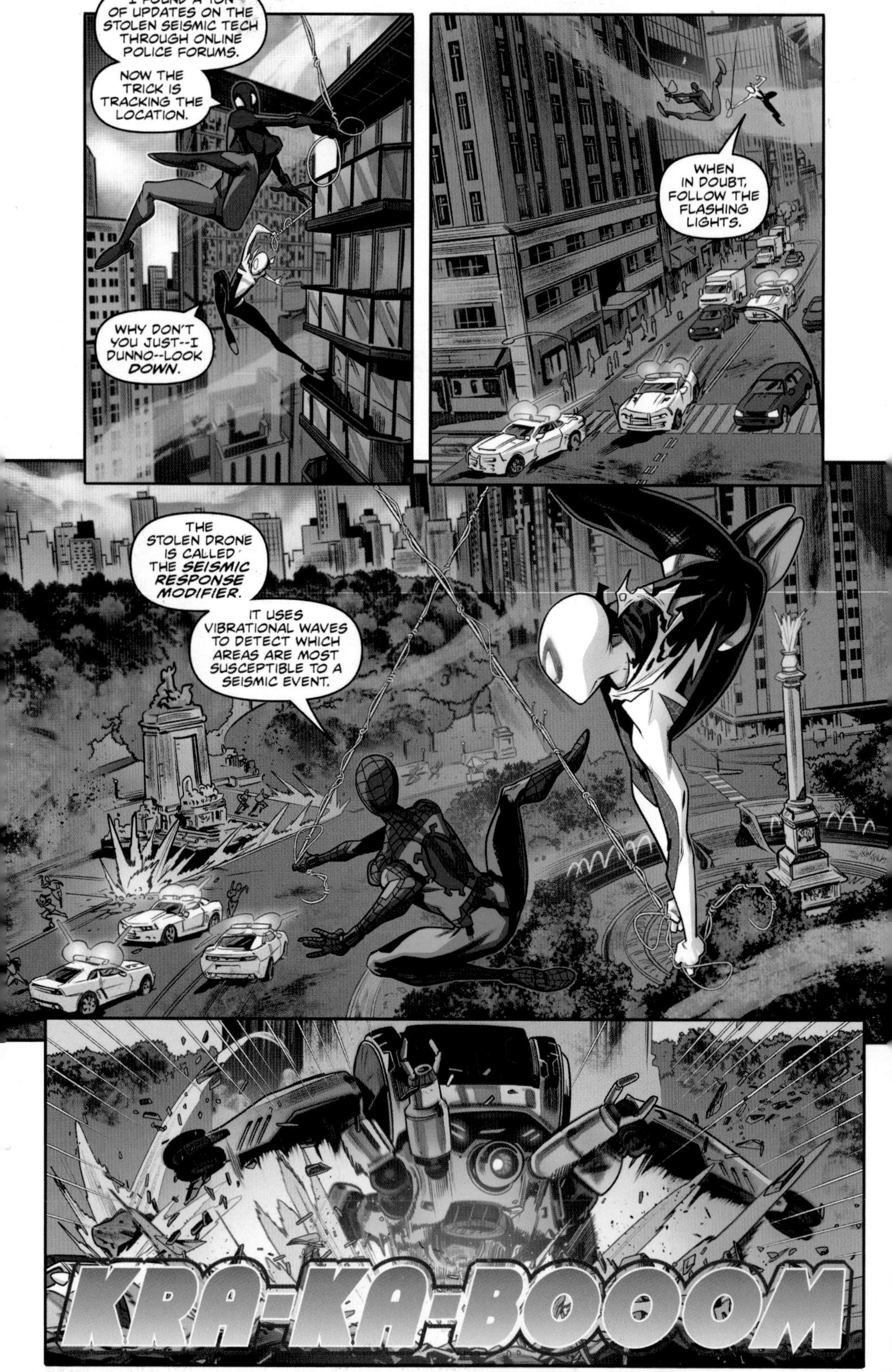
I FOUND A TON OF UPDATES ON THE STOLEN SEISMIC TECH THROUGH ONLINE POLICE FORUMS.
NOW THE TRICK IS TRACKING THE LOCATION.
WHY DON'T YOU JUST--I DUNNO--LOOK DOWN.
WHEN IN DOUBT, FOLLOW THE FLASHING LIGHTS.
THE STOLEN DRONE IS CALLED THE SEISMIC RESPONSE MODIFIER.
IT USES VIBRATIONAL WAVES TO DETECT WHICH AREAS ARE MOST SUSCEPTIBLE TO A SEISMIC EVENT.
KRA-KA-BOOOM

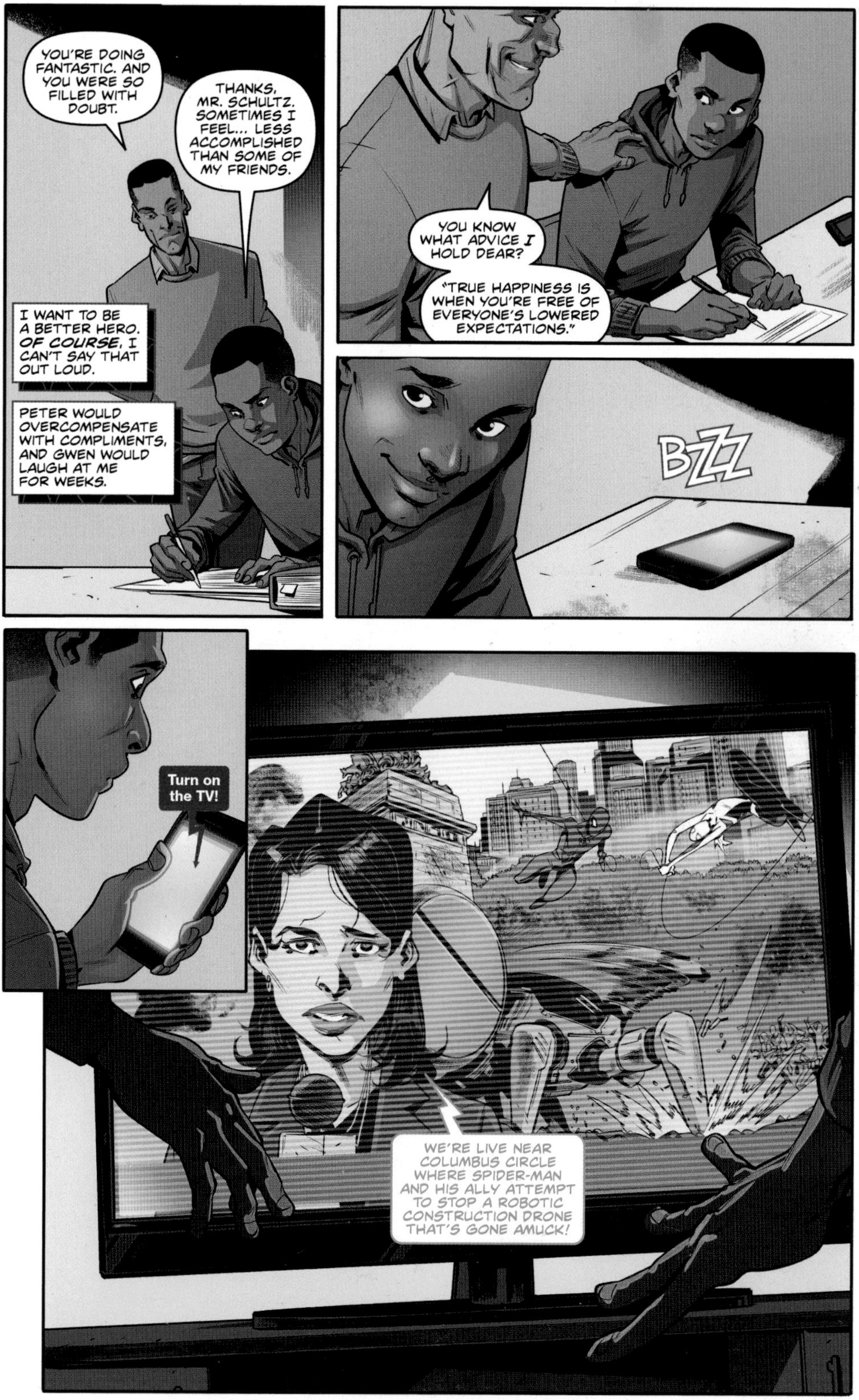
YOU'RE DOING FANTASTIC. AND YOU WERE SO FILLED WITH DOUBT.
THANKS, MR. SCHULTZ. SOMETIMES I FEEL... LESS ACCOMPLISHED THAN SOME OF MY FRIENDS.
I WANT TO BE A BETTER HERO. OF COURSE, I CAN'T SAY THAT OUT LOUD.
PETER WOULD OVERCOMPENSATE WITH COMPLIMENTS, AND GWEN WOULD LAUGH AT ME FOR WEEKS.
YOU KNOW WHAT ADVICE I HOLD DEAR?
"TRUE HAPPINESS IS WHEN YOU'RE FREE OF EVERYONE'S LOWERED EXPECTATIONS."
BZZZ
Turn on the TV!
WE'RE LIVE NEAR COLUMBUS CIRCLE WHERE SPIDER-MAN AND HIS ALLY ATTEMPT TO STOP A ROBOTIC CONSTRUCTION DRONE THAT'S GONE AMUCK!

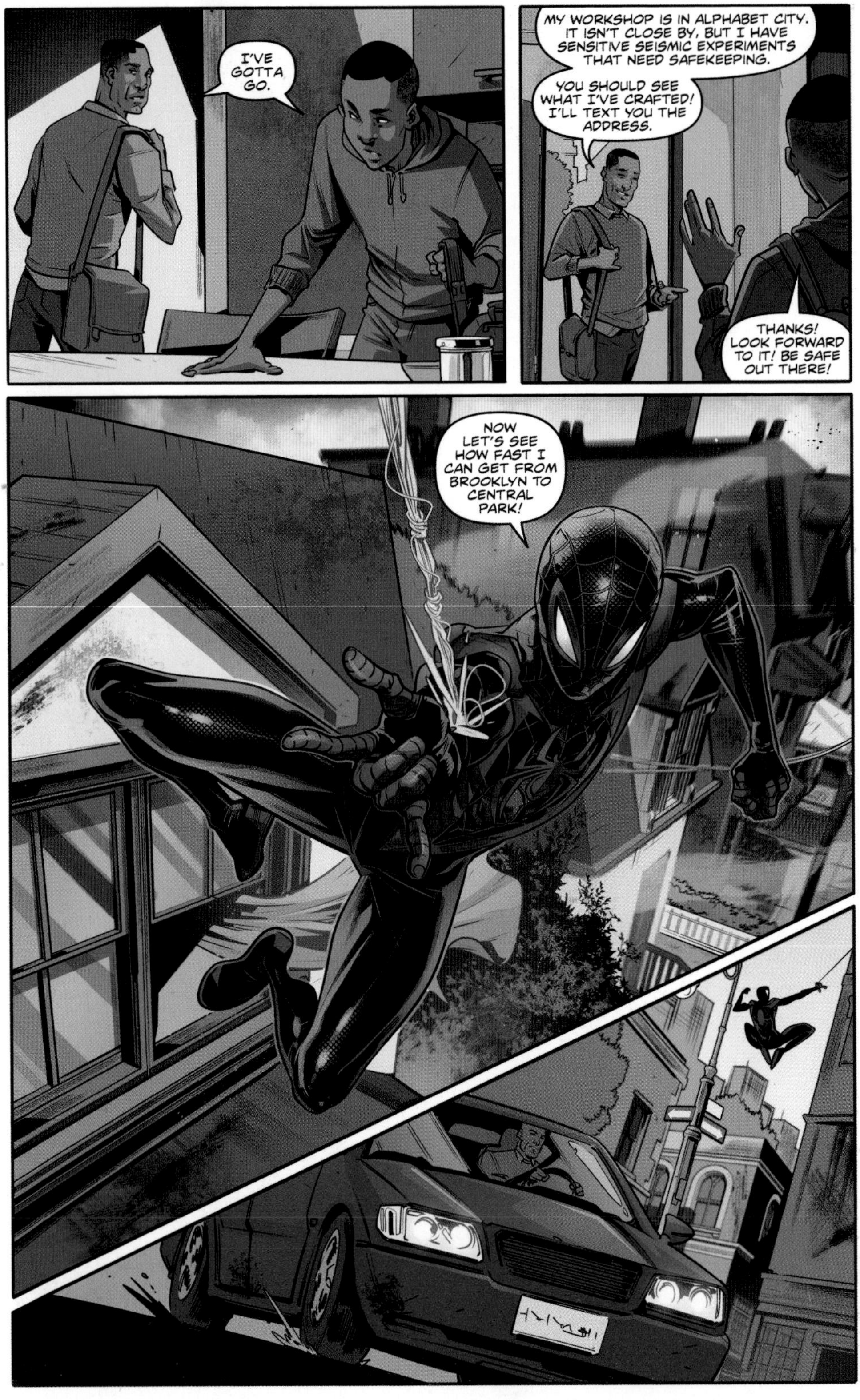
I'VE GOTTA GO.
MY WORKSHOP IS IN ALPHABET CITY. IT ISN'T CLOSE BY, BUT I HAVE SENSITIVE SEISMIC EXPERIMENTS THAT NEED SAFEKEEPING.
YOU SHOULD SEE WHAT I'VE CRAFTED! I'LL TEXT YOU THE ADDRESS.
THANKS! LOOK FORWARD TO IT! BE SAFE OUT THERE!
NOW LET'S SEE HOW FAST I CAN GET FROM BROOKLYN TO CENTRAL PARK!

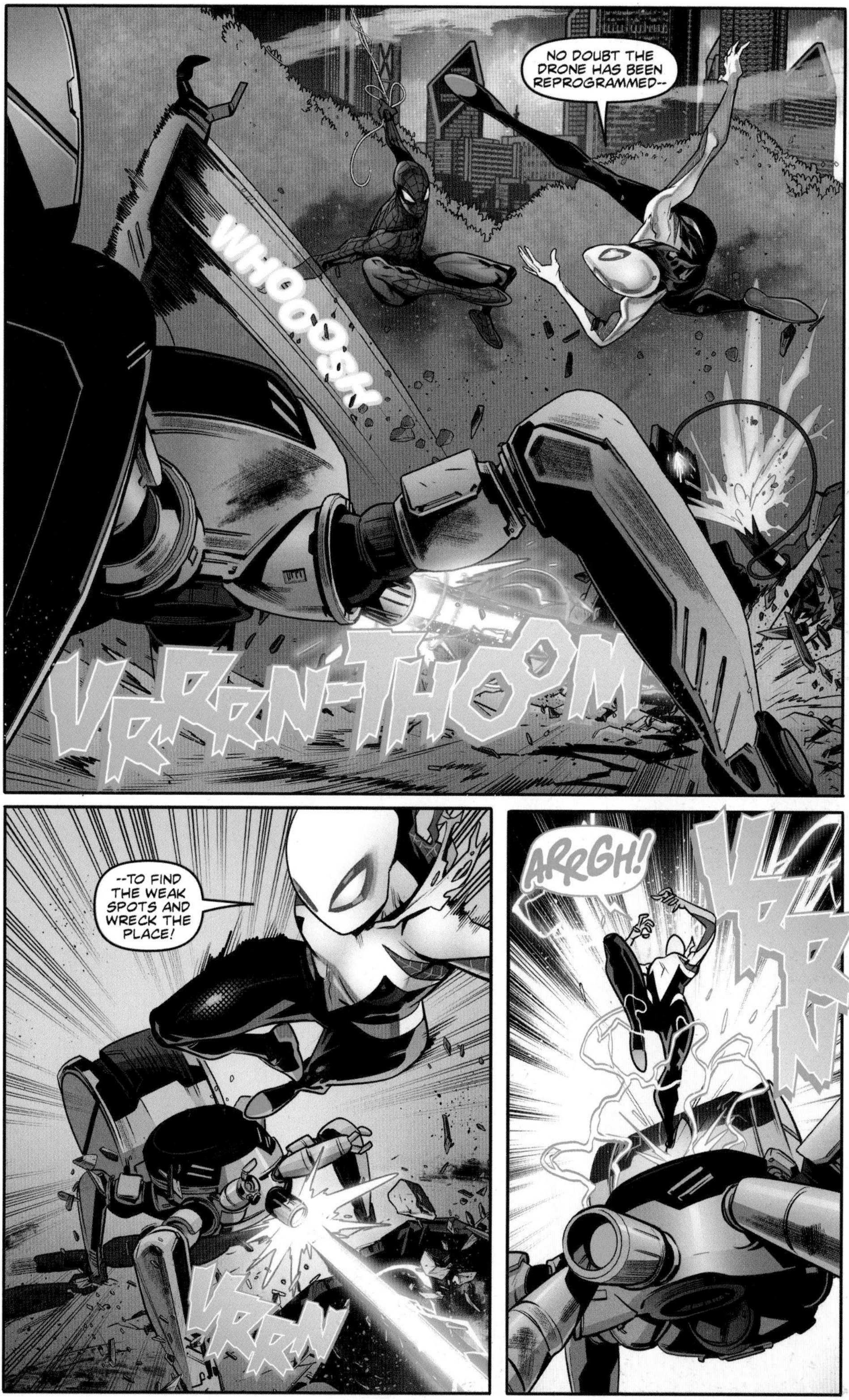
NO DOUBT THE DRONE HAS BEEN REPROGRAMMED--
WHOOOOSH
VRRRN-THOOM
--TO FIND THE WEAK SPOTS AND WRECK THE PLACE!
VRRN
ARRGH!
VRR

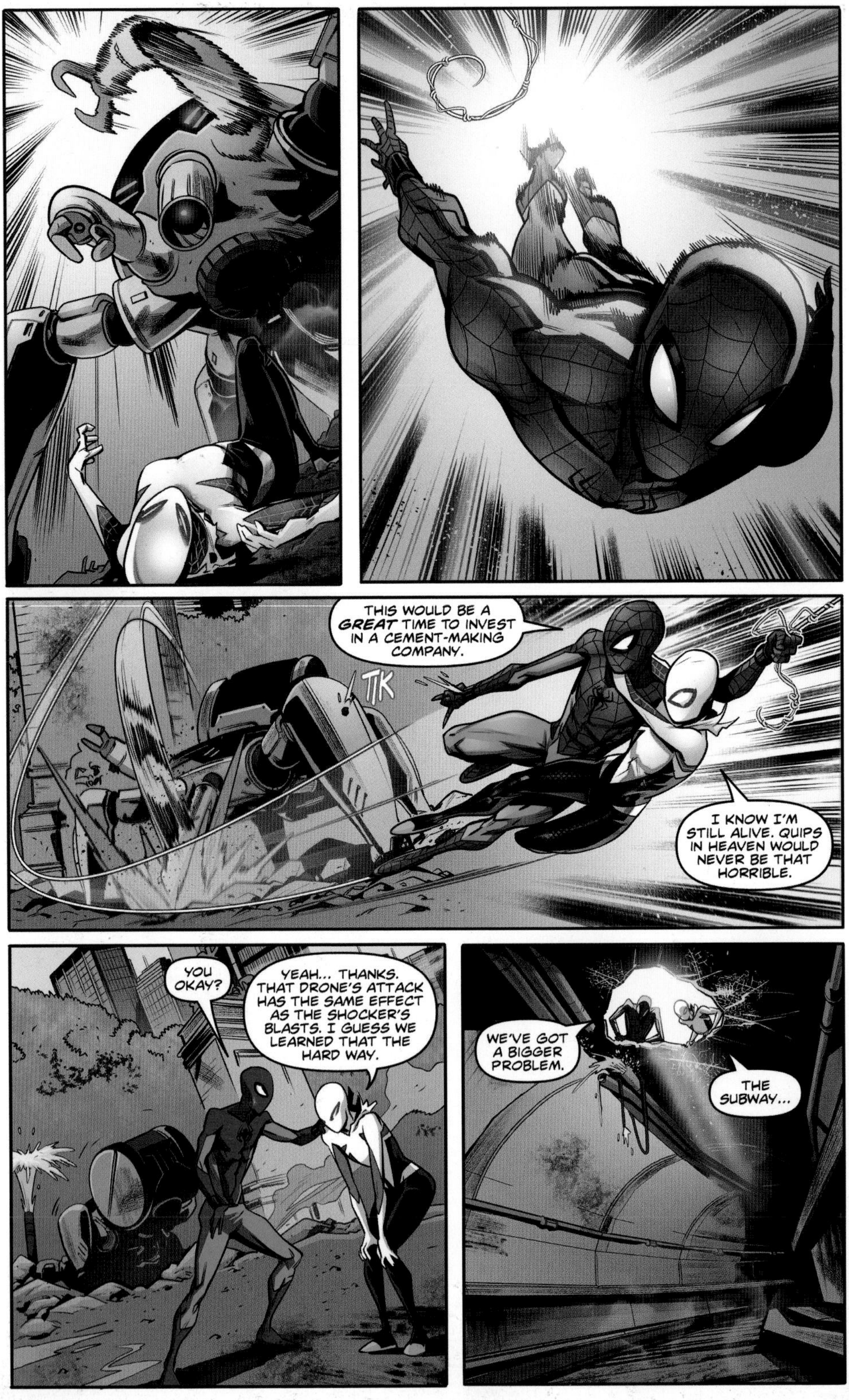
THIS WOULD BE A GREAT TIME TO INVEST IN A CEMENT-MAKING COMPANY.
TIK
I KNOW I'M STILL ALIVE. QUIPS IN HEAVEN WOULD NEVER BE THAT HORRIBLE.
YOU OKAY?
YEAH... THANKS. THAT DRONE'S ATTACK HAS THE SAME EFFECT AS THE SHOCKER'S BLASTS. I GUESS WE LEARNED THAT THE HARD WAY.
WE'VE GOT A BIGGER PROBLEM.
THE SUBWAY...

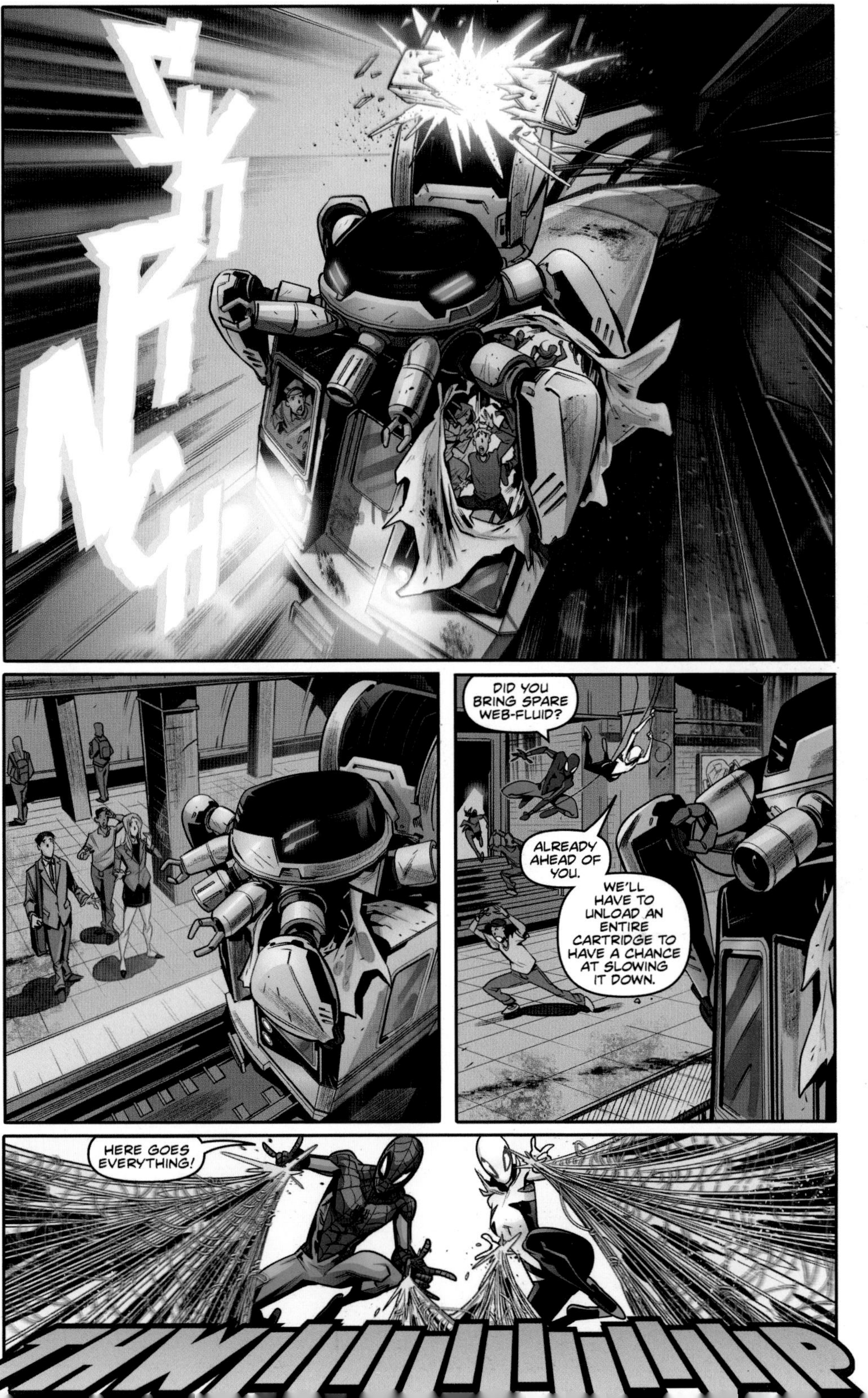
SKRANCH
DID YOU BRING SPARE WEB-FLUID?
ALREADY AHEAD OF YOU.
WE'LL HAVE TO UNLOAD AN ENTIRE CARTRIDGE TO HAVE A CHANCE AT SLOWING IT DOWN.
HERE GOES EVERYTHING!
THWIIIIIIIIIIIIP

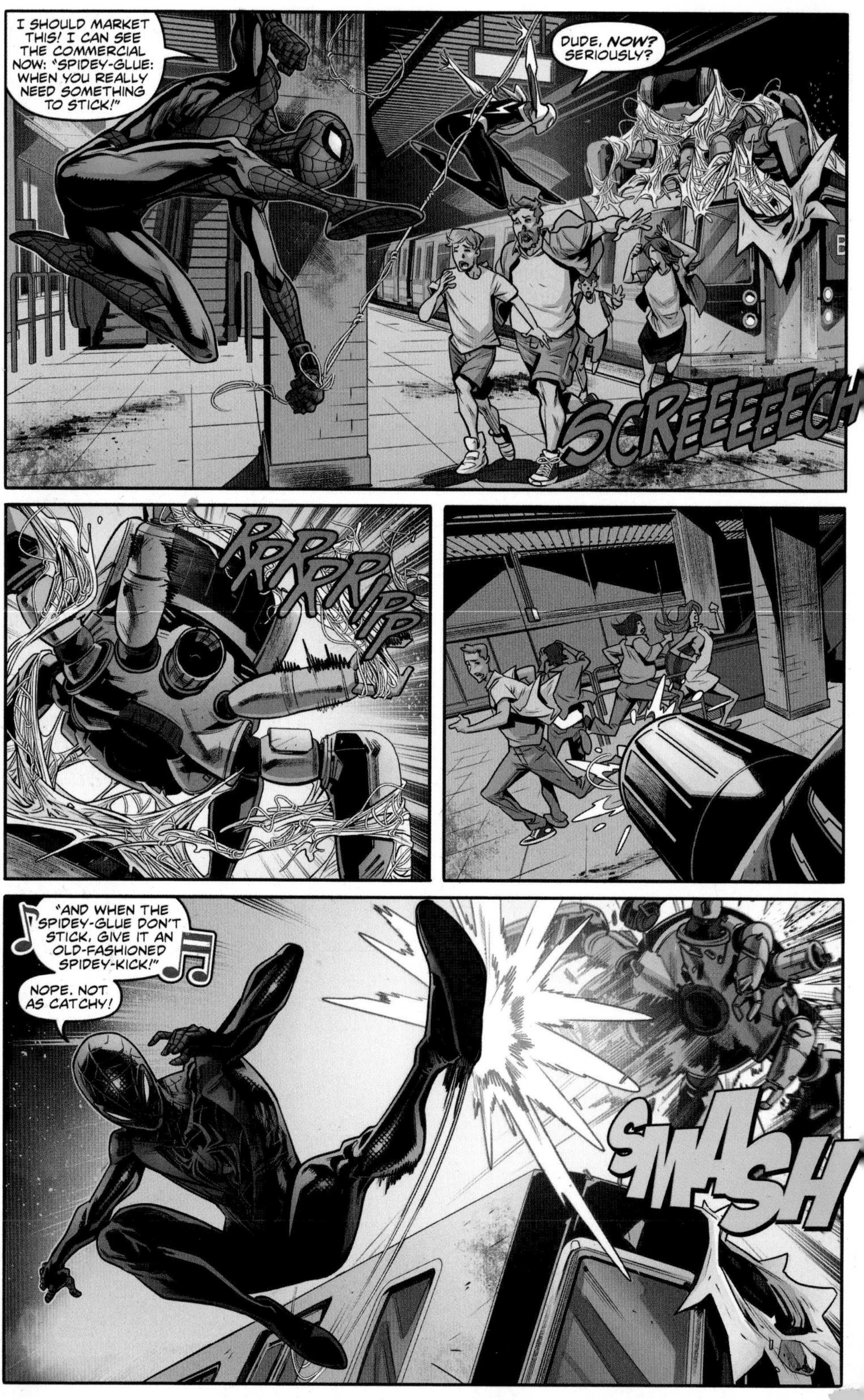
I SHOULD MARKET THIS! I CAN SEE THE COMMERCIAL NOW: "SPIDEY-GLUE: WHEN YOU REALLY NEED SOMETHING TO STICK!"
DUDE, NOW? SERIOUSLY?
SCREEEEEECH
RRRRRIPP
"AND WHEN THE SPIDEY-GLUE DON'T STICK, GIVE IT AN OLD-FASHIONED SPIDEY-KICK!"
NOPE. NOT AS CATCHY!
SMASH

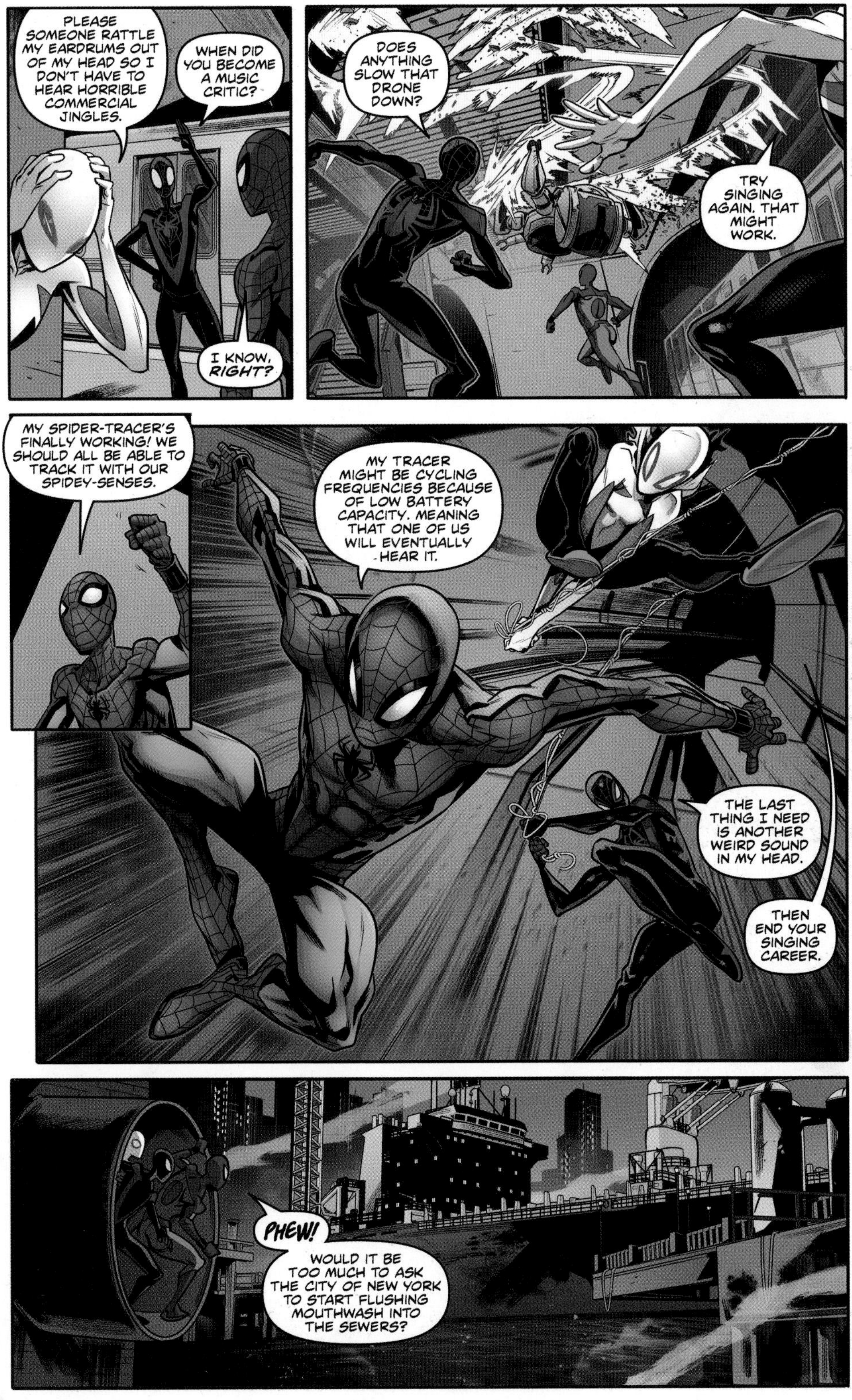
PLEASE SOMEONE RATTLE MY EARDRUMS OUT OF MY HEAD SO I DON'T HAVE TO HEAR HORRIBLE COMMERCIAL JINGLES.
WHEN DID YOU BECOME A MUSIC CRITIC?
I KNOW, RIGHT?
DOES ANYTHING SLOW THAT DRONE DOWN?
TRY SINGING AGAIN. THAT MIGHT WORK.
MY SPIDER-TRACER'S FINALLY WORKING! WE SHOULD ALL BE ABLE TO TRACK IT WITH OUR SPIDEY-SENSES.
MY TRACER MIGHT BE CYCLING FREQUENCIES BECAUSE OF LOW BATTERY CAPACITY. MEANING THAT ONE OF US WILL EVENTUALLY HEAR IT.
THE LAST THING I NEED IS ANOTHER WEIRD SOUND IN MY HEAD.
THEN END YOUR SINGING CAREER.
PHEW!
WOULD IT BE TOO MUCH TO ASK THE CITY OF NEW YORK TO START FLUSHING MOUTHWASH INTO THE SEWERS?

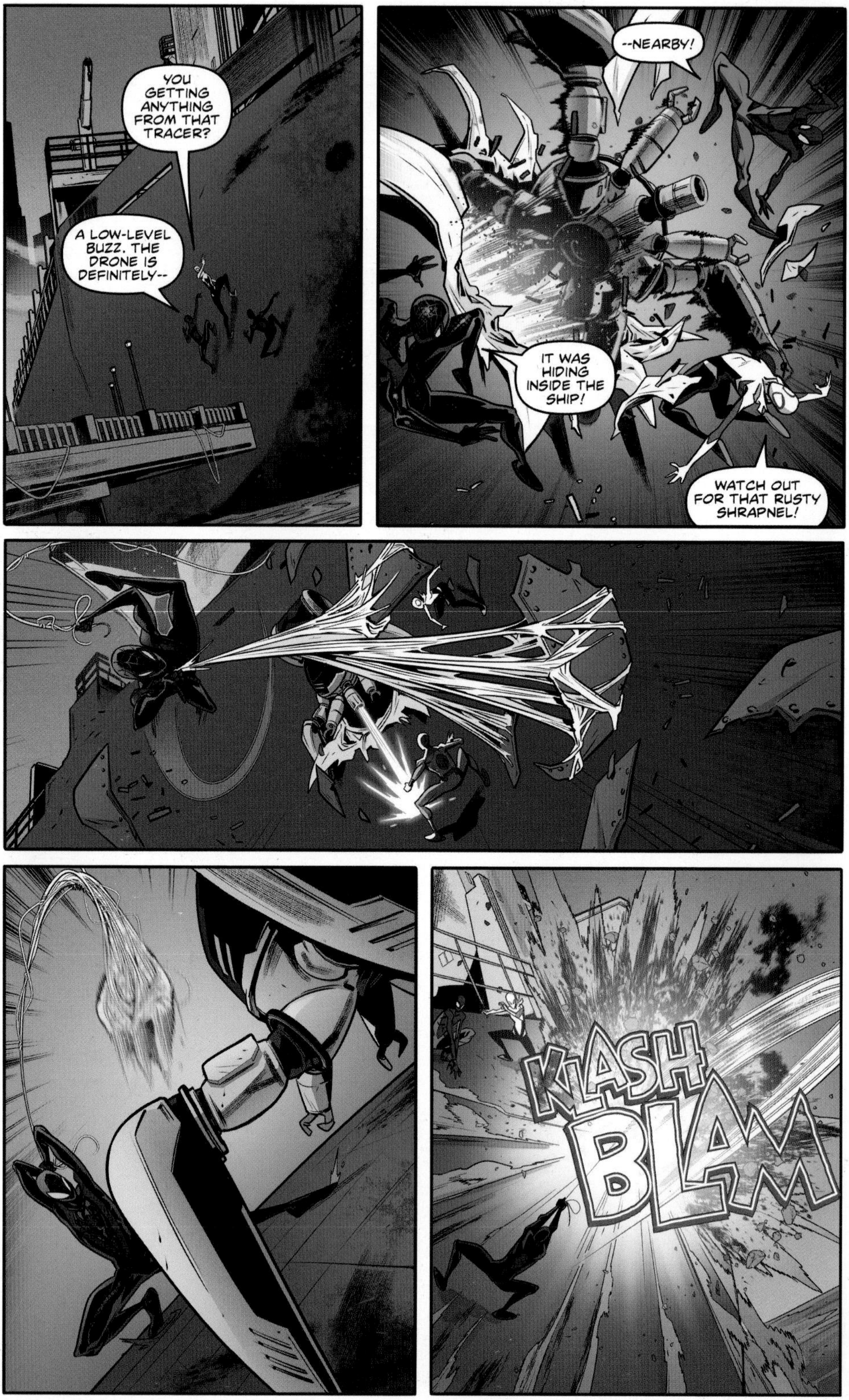
YOU GETTING ANYTHING FROM THAT TRACER?
A LOW-LEVEL BUZZ. THE DRONE IS DEFINITELY--
--NEARBY!
IT WAS HIDING INSIDE THE SHIP!
WATCH OUT FOR THAT RUSTY SHRAPNEL!
KLASH
BLAM

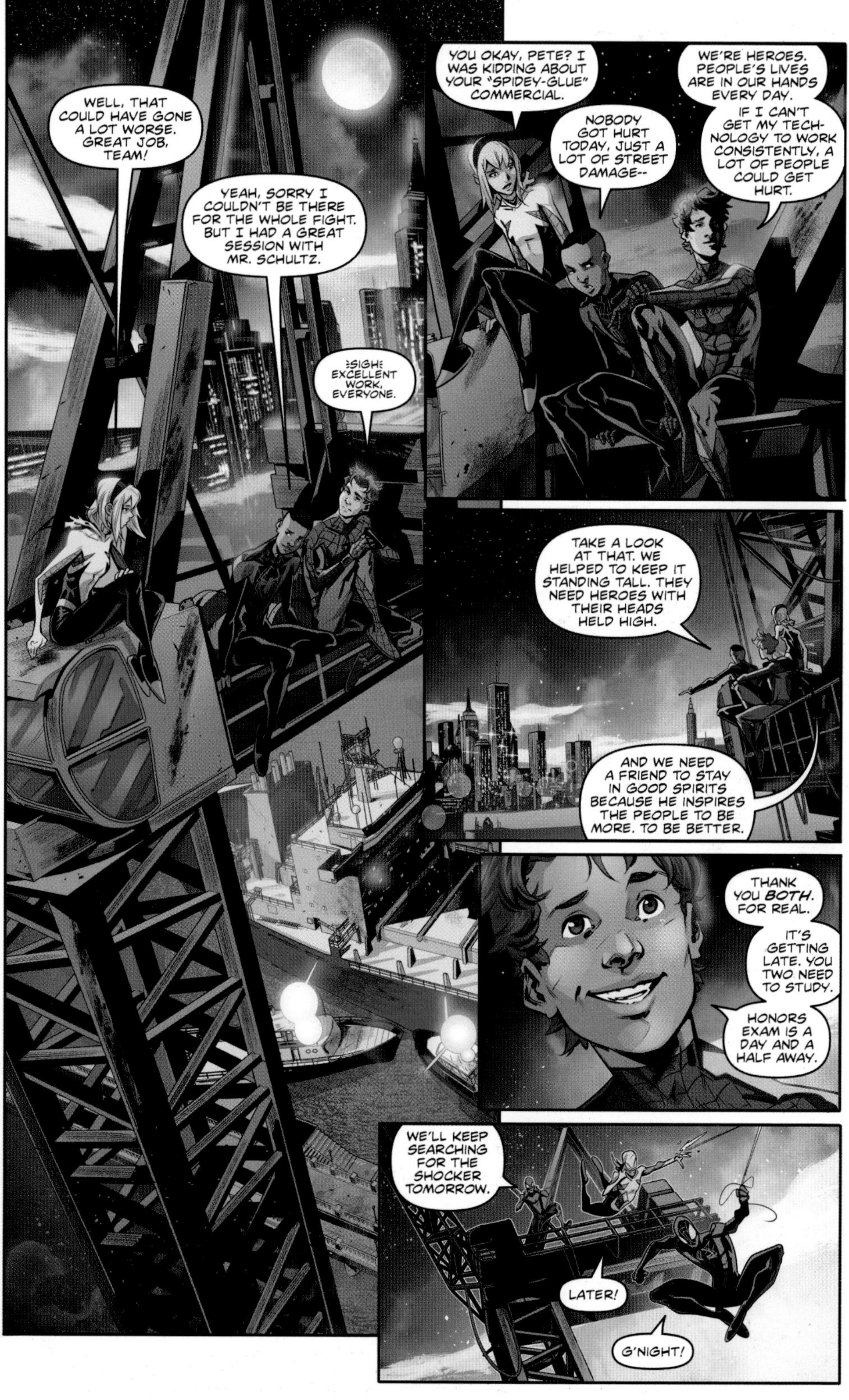
WELL, THAT COULD HAVE GONE A LOT WORSE. GREAT JOB, TEAM!
YEAH, SORRY I COULDN'T BE THERE FOR THE WHOLE FIGHT. BUT I HAD A GREAT SESSION WITH MR. SCHULTZ.
SIGH EXCELLENT WORK, EVERYONE.
YOU OKAY, PETE? I WAS KIDDING ABOUT YOUR "SPIDEY-GLUE" COMMERCIAL.
NOBODY GOT HURT TODAY, JUST A LOT OF STREET DAMAGE--
WE'RE HEROES. PEOPLE'S LIVES ARE IN OUR HANDS EVERY DAY.
IF I CAN'T GET MY TECH-NOLOGY TO WORK CONSISTENTLY, A LOT OF PEOPLE COULD GET HURT.
TAKE A LOOK AT THAT. WE HELPED TO KEEP IT STANDING TALL. THEY NEED HEROES WITH THEIR HEADS HELD HIGH.
AND WE NEED A FRIEND TO STAY IN GOOD SPIRITS BECAUSE HE INSPIRES THE PEOPLE TO BE MORE. TO BE BETTER.
THANK YOU BOTH. FOR REAL.
IT'S GETTING LATE. YOU TWO NEED TO STUDY.
HONORS EXAM IS A DAY AND A HALF AWAY.
WE'LL KEEP SEARCHING FOR THE SHOCKER TOMORROW.
LATER!
G'NIGHT!

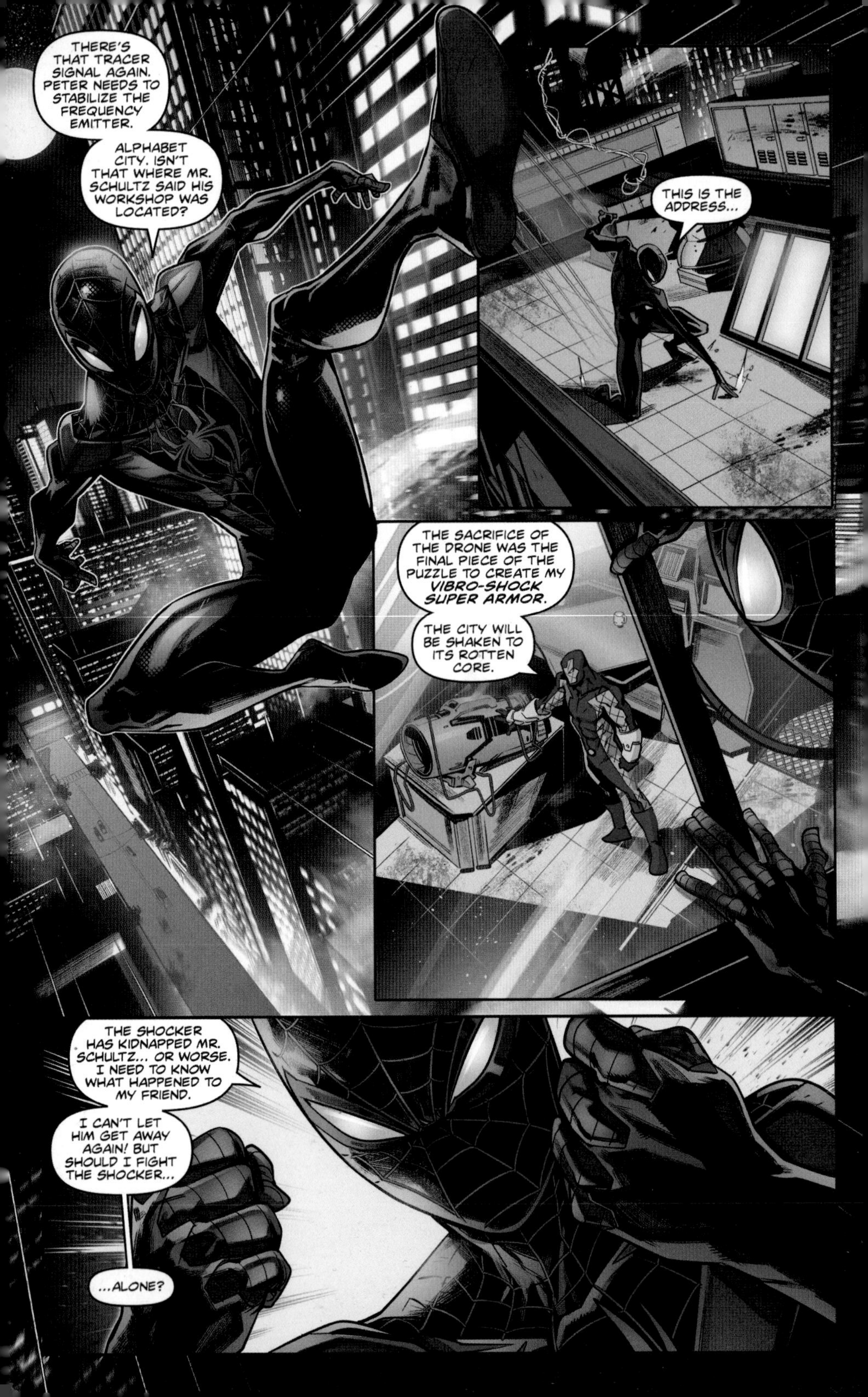
THERE'S THAT TRACER SIGNAL AGAIN. PETER NEEDS TO STABILIZE THE FREQUENCY EMITTER.
ALPHABET CITY. ISN'T THAT WHERE MR. SCHULTZ SAID HIS WORKSHOP WAS LOCATED?
THIS IS THE ADDRESS...
THE SACRIFICE OF THE DRONE WAS THE FINAL PIECE OF THE PUZZLE TO CREATE MY *VIBRO-SHOCK SUPER ARMOR*.
THE CITY WILL BE SHAKEN TO ITS ROTTEN CORE.
THE SHOCKER HAS KIDNAPPED MR. SCHULTZ... OR WORSE. I NEED TO KNOW WHAT HAPPENED TO MY FRIEND.
I CAN'T LET HIM GET AWAY AGAIN! BUT SHOULD I FIGHT THE SHOCKER...
...ALONE?

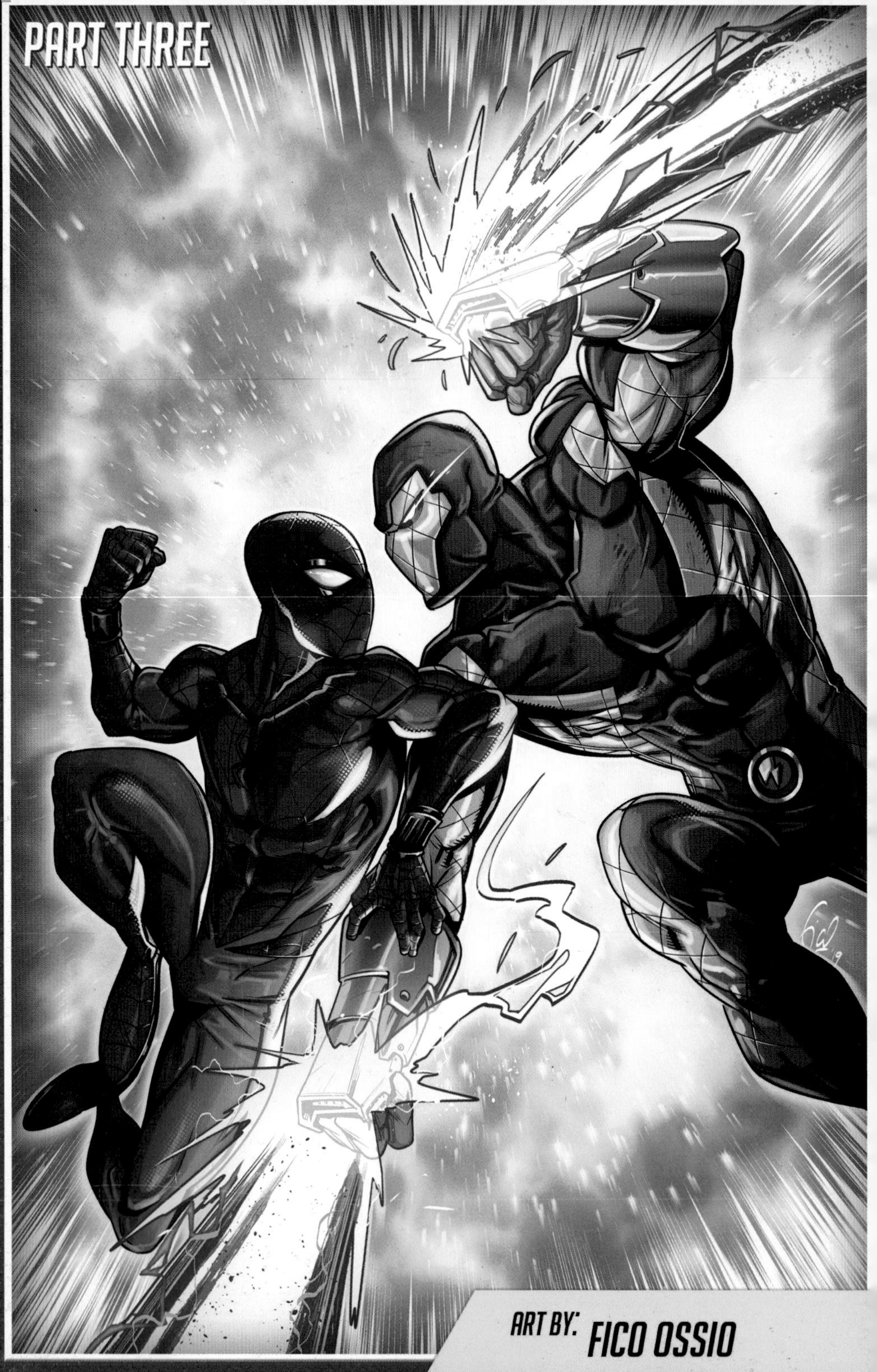
PART THREE
ART BY: FICO OSSIO

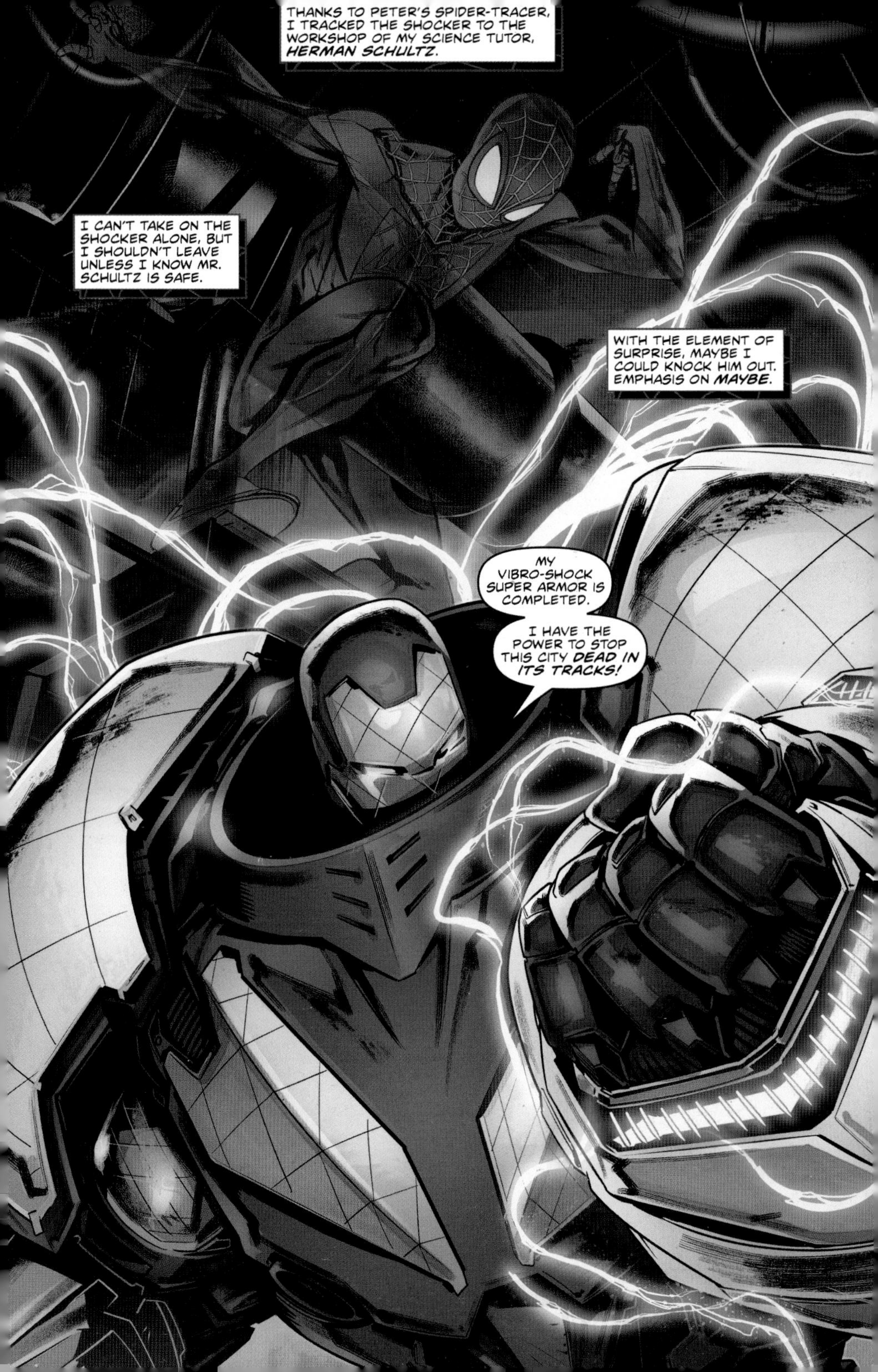
THANKS TO PETER'S SPIDER-TRACER, I TRACKED THE SHOCKER TO THE WORKSHOP OF MY SCIENCE TUTOR, HERMAN SCHULTZ.
I CAN'T TAKE ON THE SHOCKER ALONE, BUT I SHOULDN'T LEAVE UNLESS I KNOW MR. SCHULTZ IS SAFE.
WITH THE ELEMENT OF SURPRISE, MAYBE I COULD KNOCK HIM OUT. EMPHASIS ON MAYBE.
MY VIBRO-SHOCK SUPER ARMOR IS COMPLETED.
I HAVE THE POWER TO STOP THIS CITY DEAD IN ITS TRACKS!

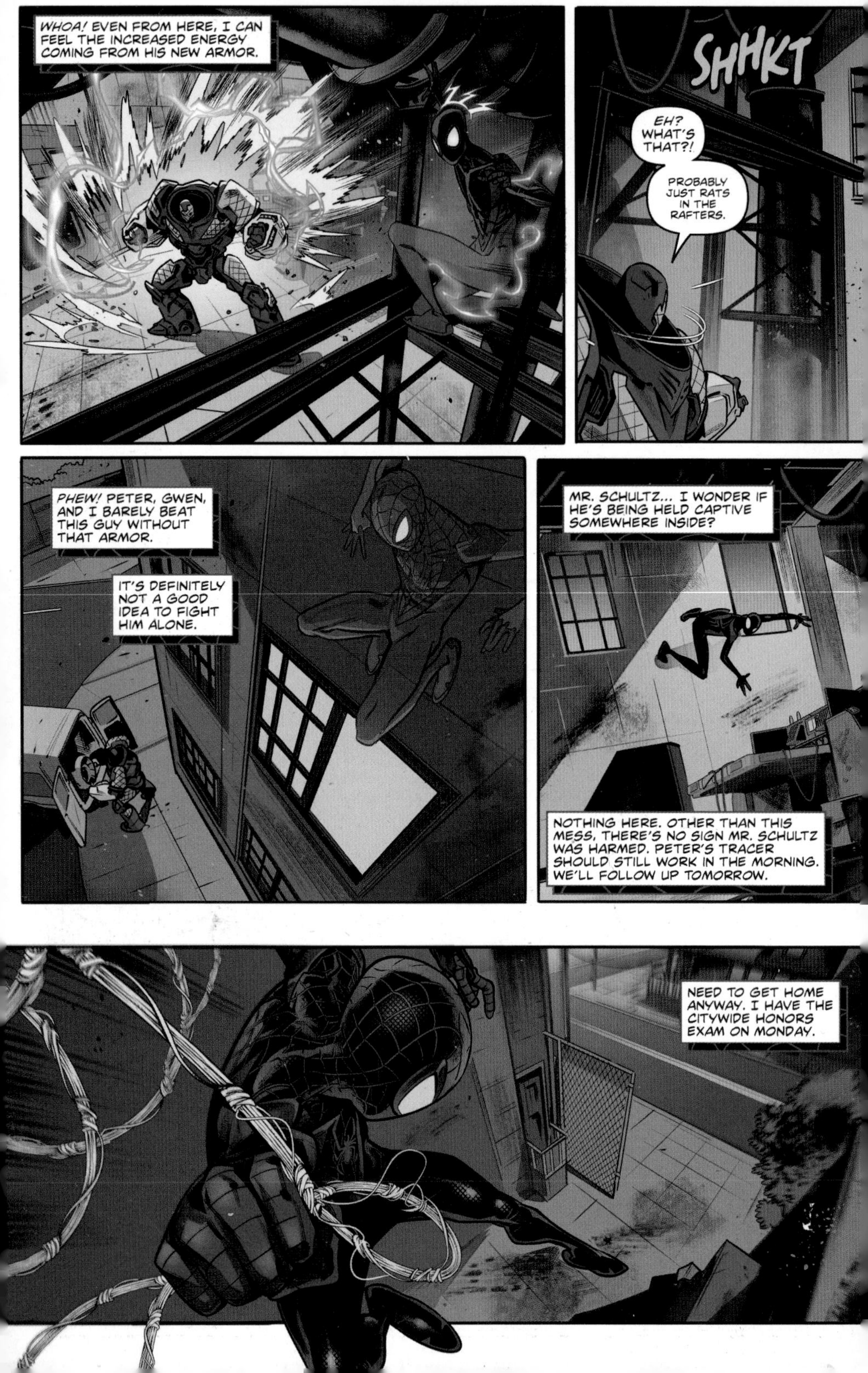
WHOA! EVEN FROM HERE, I CAN FEEL THE INCREASED ENERGY COMING FROM HIS NEW ARMOR.
SHHKT
EH? WHAT'S THAT?!
PROBABLY JUST RATS IN THE RAFTERS.
PHEW! PETER, GWEN, AND I BARELY BEAT THIS GUY WITHOUT THAT ARMOR.
IT'S DEFINITELY NOT A GOOD IDEA TO FIGHT HIM ALONE.
MR. SCHULTZ... I WONDER IF HE'S BEING HELD CAPTIVE SOMEWHERE INSIDE?
NOTHING HERE. OTHER THAN THIS MESS, THERE'S NO SIGN MR. SCHULTZ WAS HARMED. PETER'S TRACER SHOULD STILL WORK IN THE MORNING. WE'LL FOLLOW UP TOMORROW.
NEED TO GET HOME ANYWAY. I HAVE THE CITYWIDE HONORS EXAM ON MONDAY.

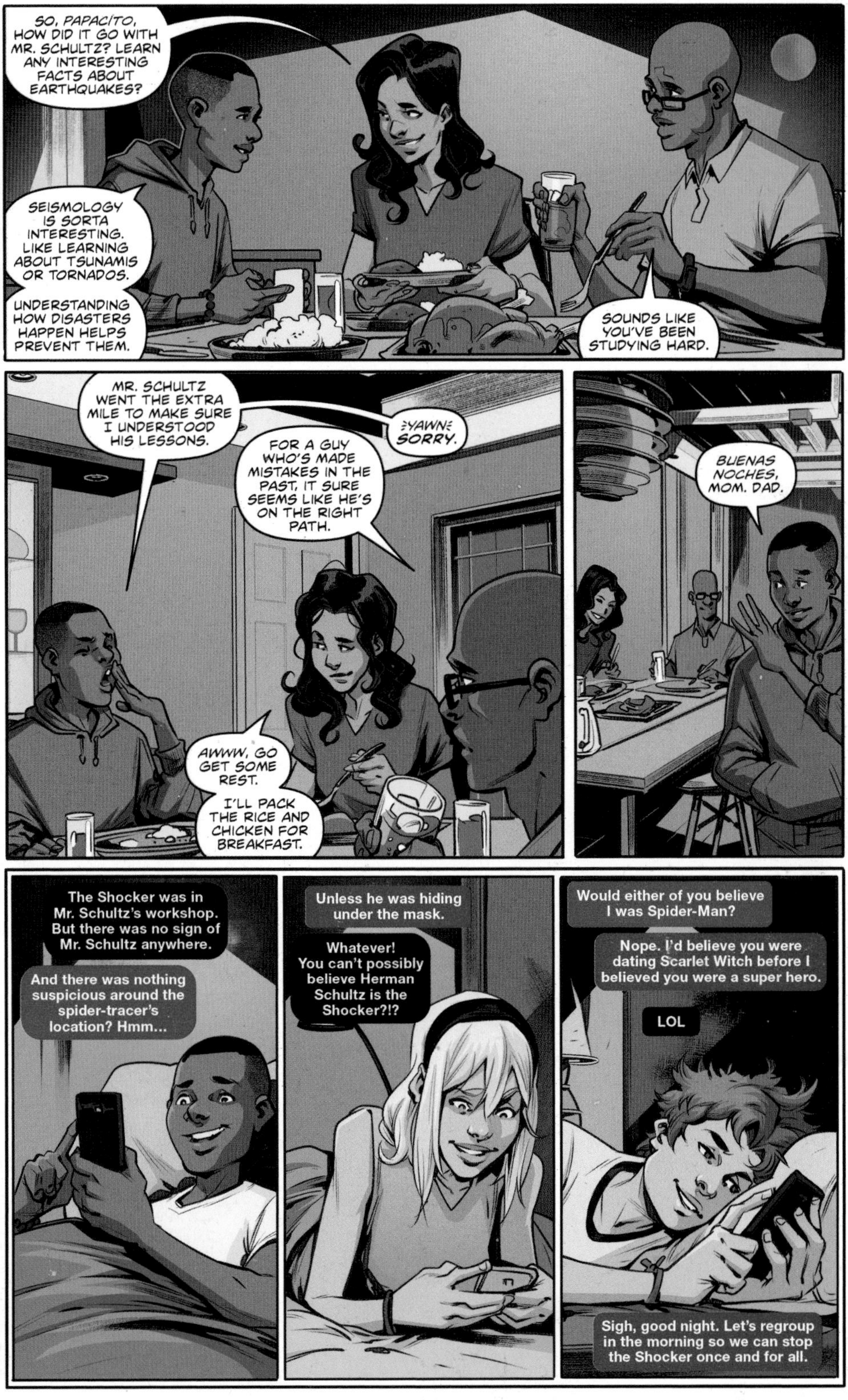
SO, PAPACITO, HOW DID IT GO WITH MR. SCHULTZ? LEARN ANY INTERESTING FACTS ABOUT EARTHQUAKES?
SEISMOLOGY IS SORTA INTERESTING. LIKE LEARNING ABOUT TSUNAMIS OR TORNADOS.
UNDERSTANDING HOW DISASTERS HAPPEN HELPS PREVENT THEM.
SOUNDS LIKE YOU'VE BEEN STUDYING HARD.
MR. SCHULTZ WENT THE EXTRA MILE TO MAKE SURE I UNDERSTOOD HIS LESSONS.
FOR A GUY WHO'S MADE MISTAKES IN THE PAST, IT SURE SEEMS LIKE HE'S ON THE RIGHT PATH.
YAWN SORRY.
AWWW, GO GET SOME REST.
I'LL PACK THE RICE AND CHICKEN FOR BREAKFAST.
BUENAS NOCHES, MOM. DAD.
The Shocker was in Mr. Schultz's workshop. But there was no sign of Mr. Schultz anywhere.
And there was nothing suspicious around the spider-tracer's location? Hmm...
Unless he was hiding under the mask.
Whatever! You can't possibly believe Herman Schultz is the Shocker?!?
Would either of you believe I was Spider-Man?
Nope. I'd believe you were dating Scarlet Witch before I believed you were a super hero.
LOL
Sigh, good night. Let's regroup in the morning so we can stop the Shocker once and for all.

IT SEEMS THAT THE SHOCKER'S ARMOR HAS SIMILAR *POWER DISTRIBUTION* PROBLEMS AS MY SPIDER-TRACERS.

SHOULD I TELL MOM THAT I'M REALLY NOT IN THE MOOD FOR RICE AND CHICKEN FIRST THING IN THE MORNING?

*UH, PERSONAL SPACE, LADY?*

MILES TOLD ME HE STILL HASN'T RETURNED THAT BOOK ON TECTONIC ALIGNMENT.

Is there any way you can swing over to the 42nd street branch? You know, return the last available book in the city on tectonic plates.

Yeah, no problem. I'll bring it when we connect to search for the Shocker.

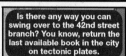

Gotta run! Talk later!

GOOD MORNING, MILES! CAN I COME IN?

*UH--GIMME ONE SECOND! PUTTING ON MY PANTS!*

HERE'S THE REST OF LAST NIGHT'S DINNER. A HEALTHY BRAIN NEEDS HEALTHY FUEL.

YOU GOT A MINUTE? I NEED TO TALK TO YOU ABOUT SOMETHING.

I ALWAYS HAVE TIME FOR YOU.

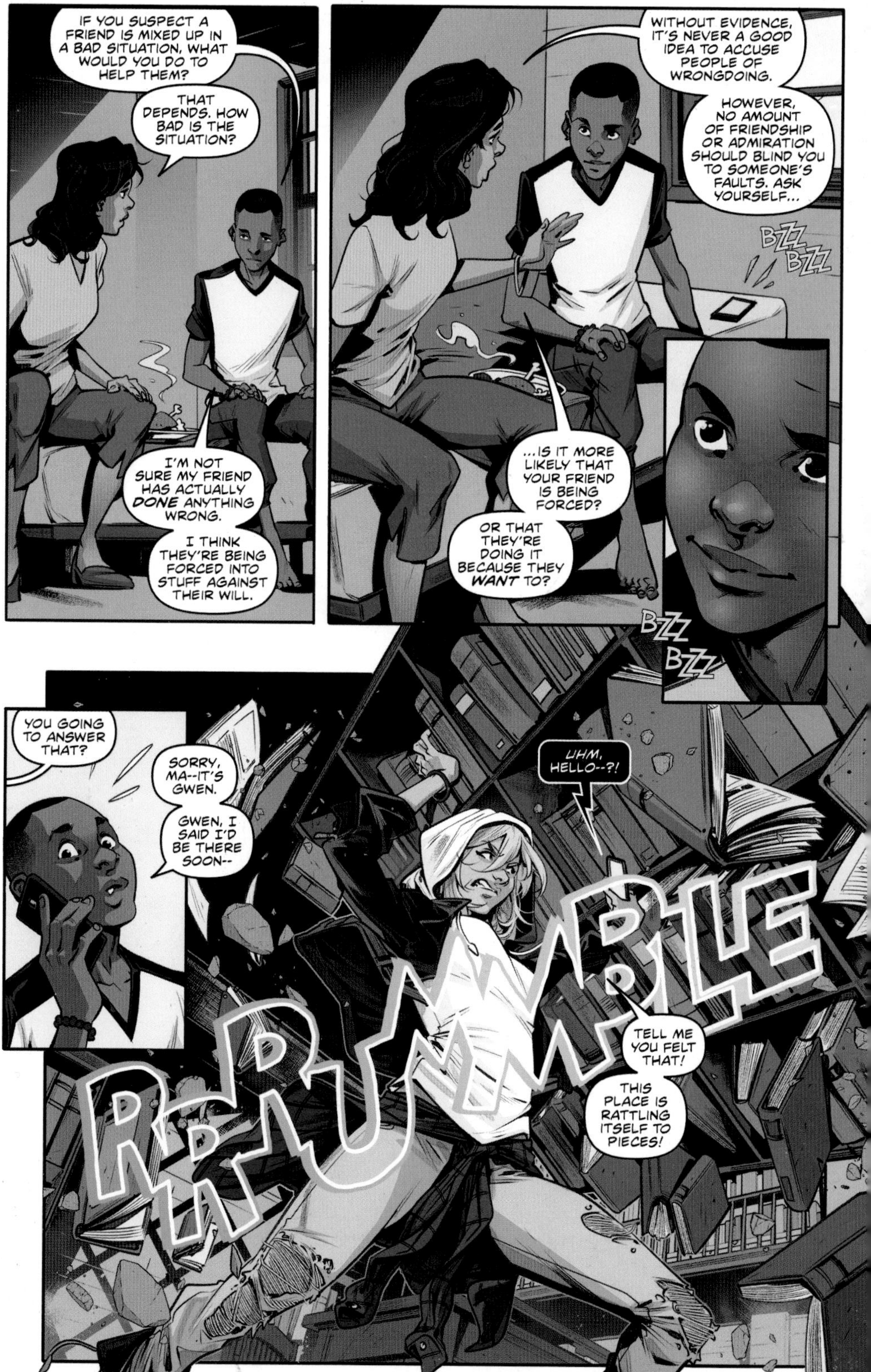
IF YOU SUSPECT A FRIEND IS MIXED UP IN A BAD SITUATION, WHAT WOULD YOU DO TO HELP THEM?
THAT DEPENDS. HOW BAD IS THE SITUATION?
I'M NOT SURE MY FRIEND HAS ACTUALLY DONE ANYTHING WRONG.
I THINK THEY'RE BEING FORCED INTO STUFF AGAINST THEIR WILL.
WITHOUT EVIDENCE, IT'S NEVER A GOOD IDEA TO ACCUSE PEOPLE OF WRONGDOING.
HOWEVER, NO AMOUNT OF FRIENDSHIP OR ADMIRATION SHOULD BLIND YOU TO SOMEONE'S FAULTS. ASK YOURSELF...
BZZZ BZZZ
...IS IT MORE LIKELY THAT YOUR FRIEND IS BEING FORCED?
OR THAT THEY'RE DOING IT BECAUSE THEY WANT TO?
BZZZ BZZZ
YOU GOING TO ANSWER THAT?
SORRY, MA--IT'S GWEN.
GWEN, I SAID I'D BE THERE SOON--
UHM, HELLO--?!
RRRUMMBLE
TELL ME YOU FELT THAT!
THIS PLACE IS RATTLING ITSELF TO PIECES!

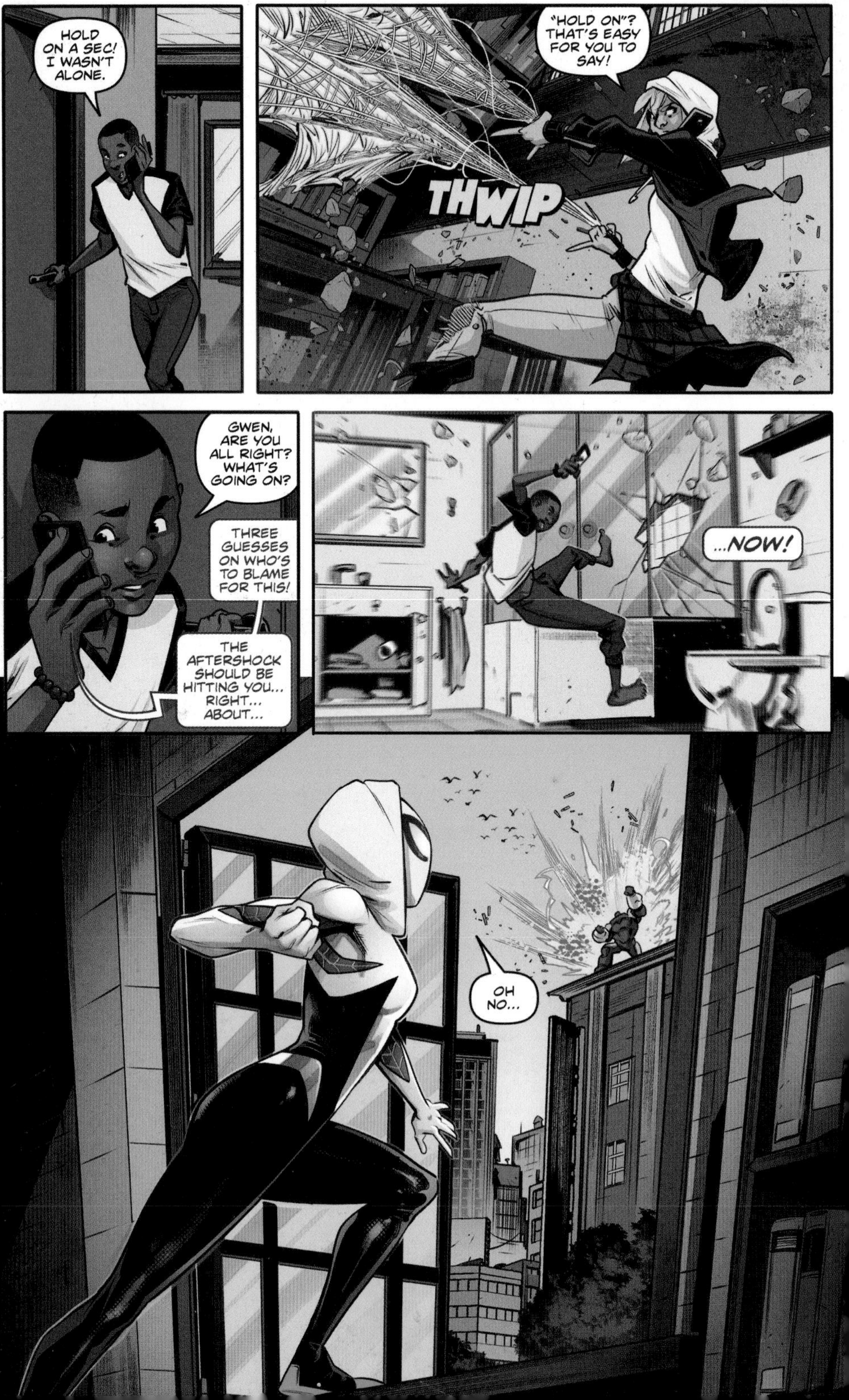
HOLD ON A SEC! I WASN'T ALONE.
"HOLD ON"? THAT'S EASY FOR YOU TO SAY!
THWIP
GWEN, ARE YOU ALL RIGHT? WHAT'S GOING ON?
THREE GUESSES ON WHO'S TO BLAME FOR THIS!
THE AFTERSHOCK SHOULD BE HITTING YOU... RIGHT... ABOUT...
...NOW!
OH NO...

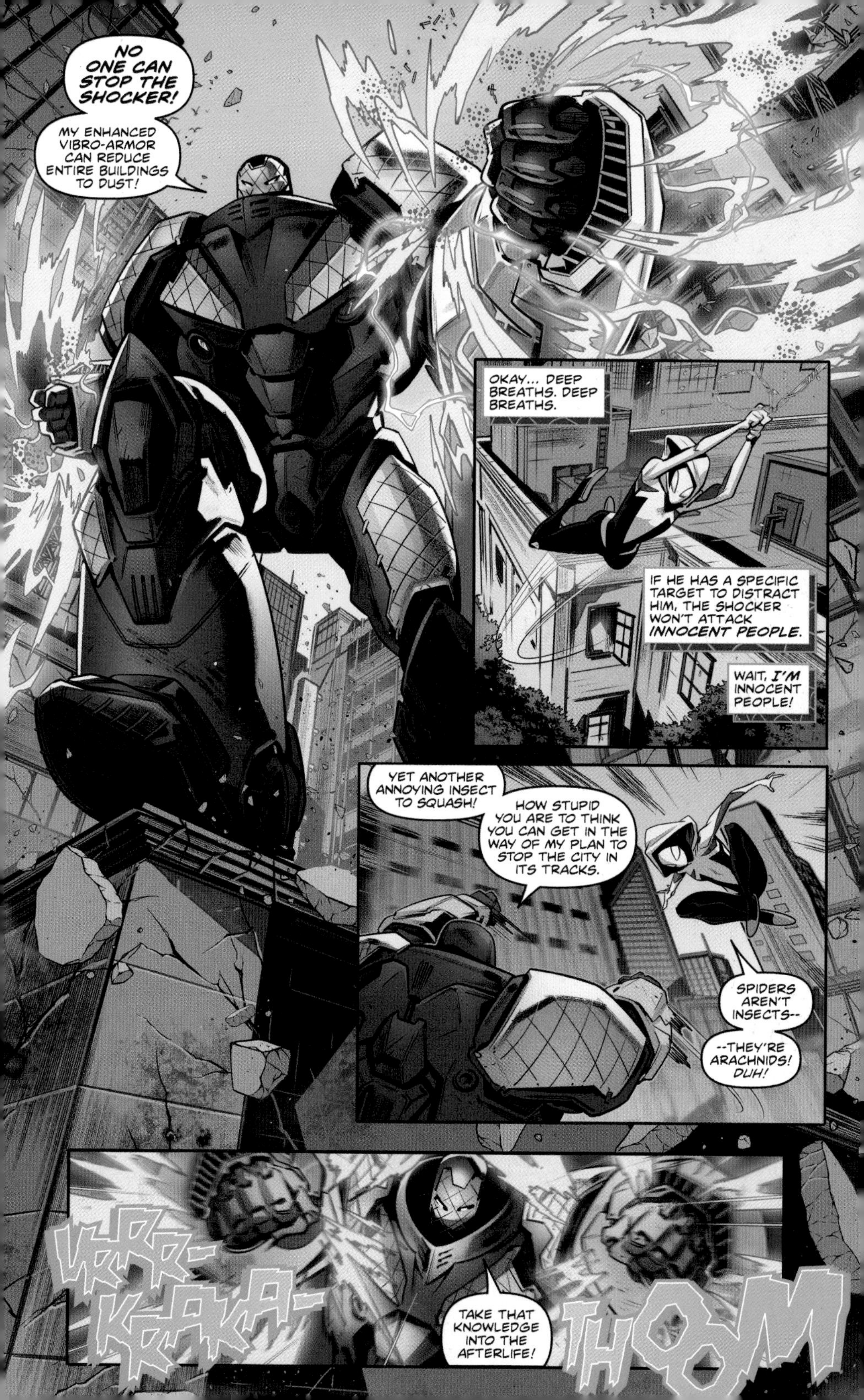
NO ONE CAN STOP THE SHOCKER!
MY ENHANCED VIBRO-ARMOR CAN REDUCE ENTIRE BUILDINGS TO DUST!
OKAY... DEEP BREATHS. DEEP BREATHS.
IF HE HAS A SPECIFIC TARGET TO DISTRACT HIM, THE SHOCKER WON'T ATTACK INNOCENT PEOPLE.
WAIT, I'M INNOCENT PEOPLE!
YET ANOTHER ANNOYING INSECT TO SQUASH!
HOW STUPID YOU ARE TO THINK YOU CAN GET IN THE WAY OF MY PLAN TO STOP THE CITY IN ITS TRACKS.
SPIDERS AREN'T INSECTS--
--THEY'RE ARACHNIDS! DUH!
VRR-KRAKA-THOOM
TAKE THAT KNOWLEDGE INTO THE AFTERLIFE!

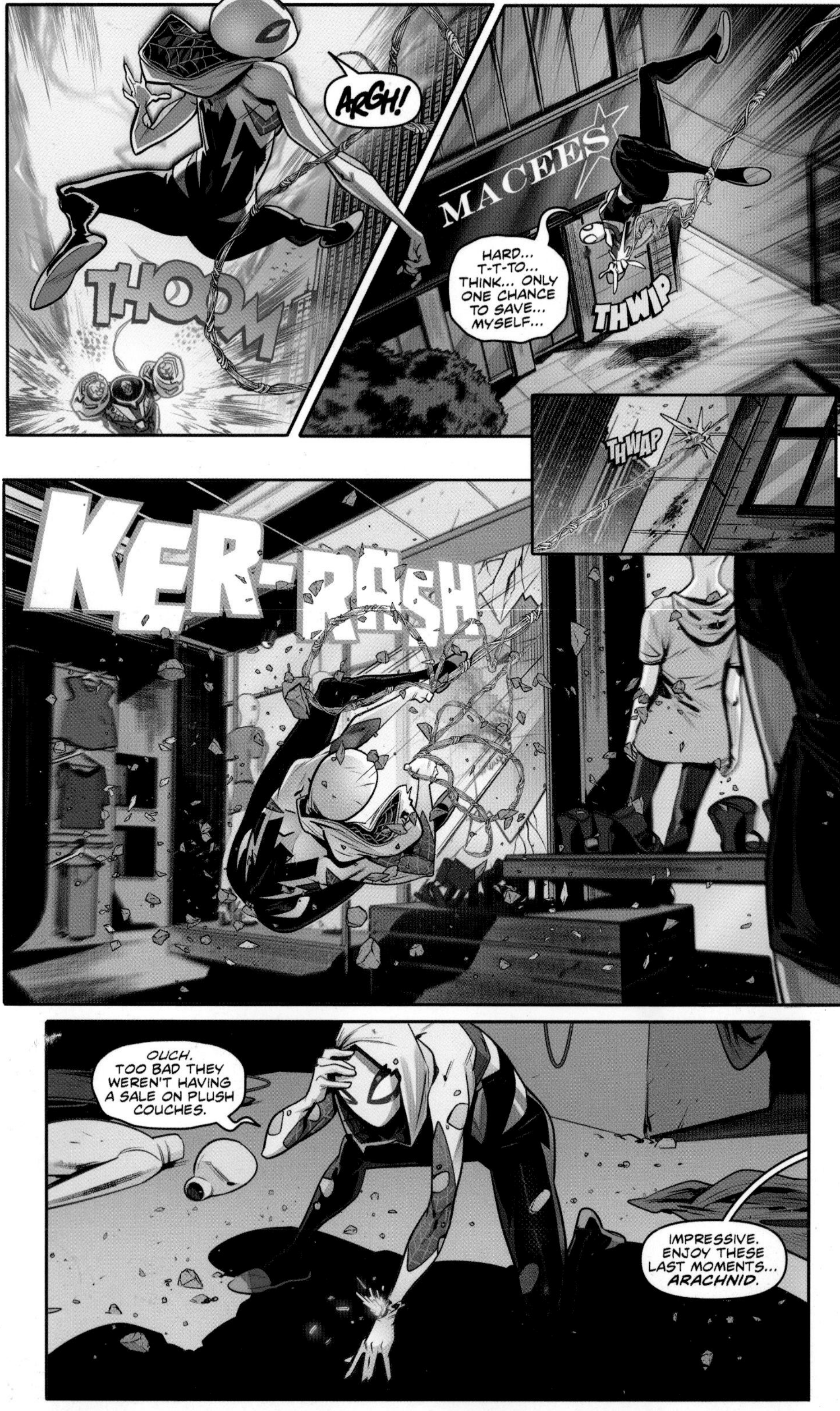
ARGH!
THOOM
MACEES
HARD... T-T-TO... THINK... ONLY ONE CHANCE TO SAVE... MYSELF...
THWIP
THWAP
KER-RASH
OUCH. TOO BAD THEY WEREN'T HAVING A SALE ON PLUSH COUCHES.
IMPRESSIVE. ENJOY THESE LAST MOMENTS... ARACHNID.

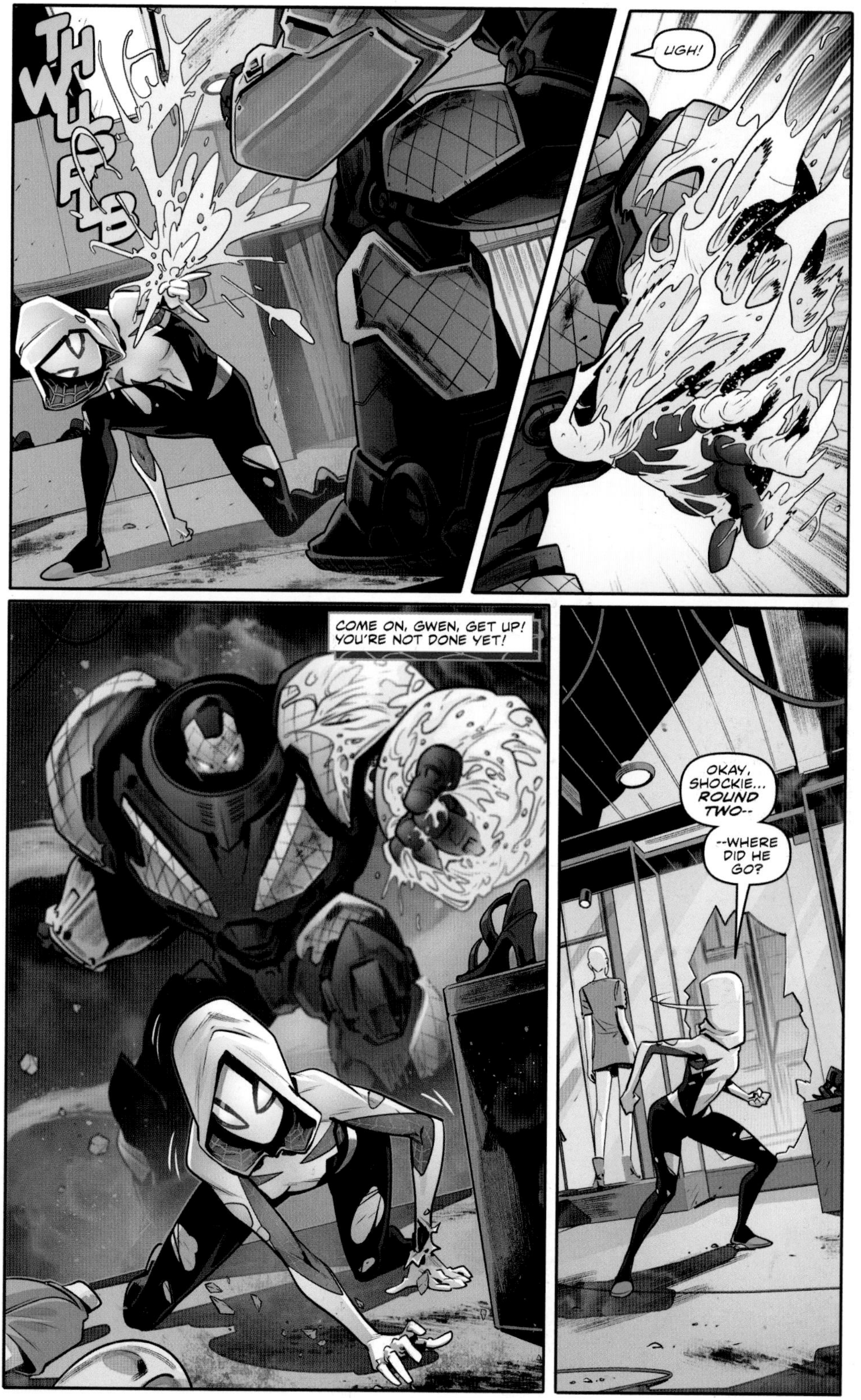
UGH!
COME ON, GWEN, GET UP! YOU'RE NOT DONE YET!
OKAY, SHOCKIE... ROUND TWO--
--WHERE DID HE GO?

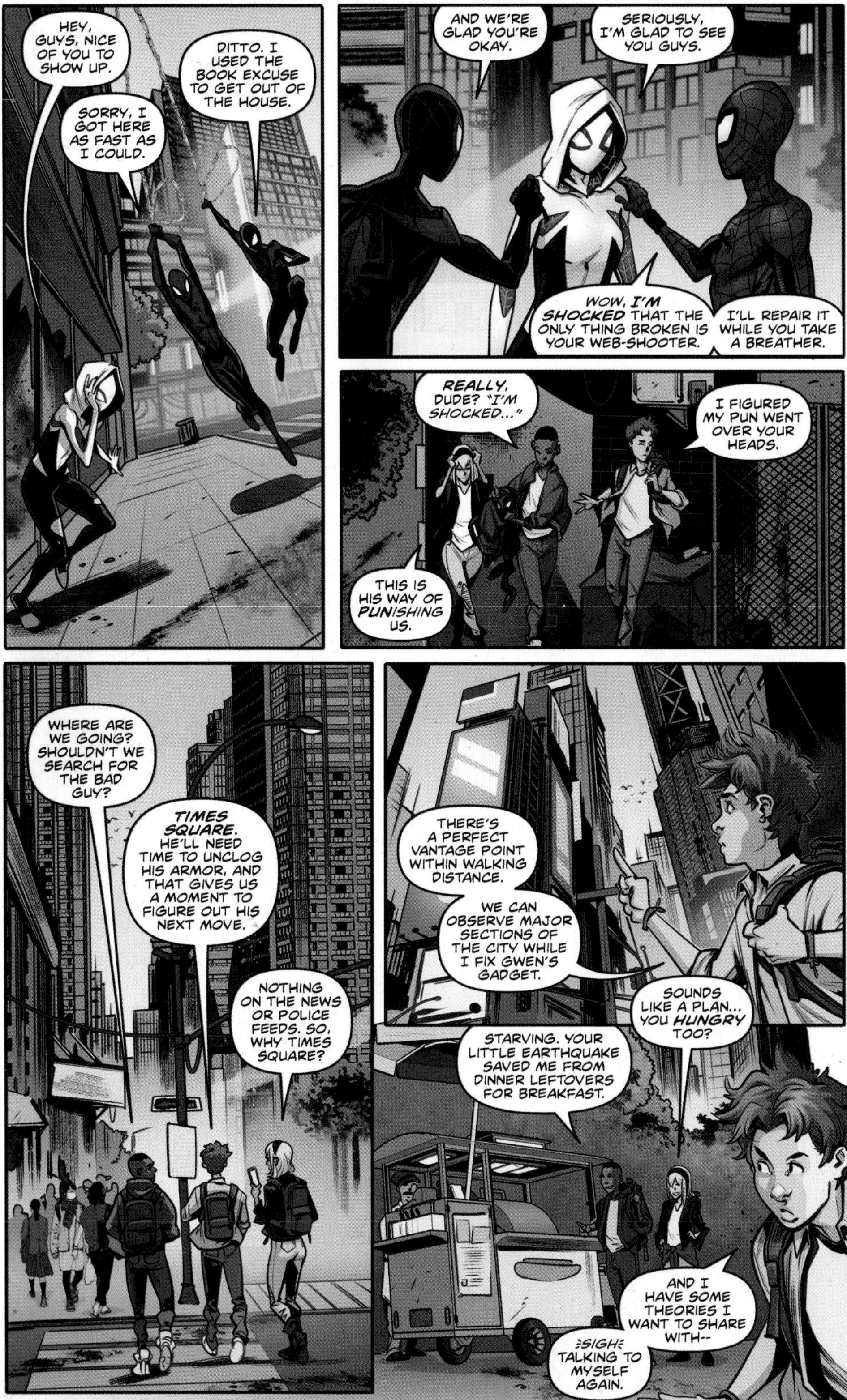
HEY, GUYS, NICE OF YOU TO SHOW UP.
SORRY, I GOT HERE AS FAST AS I COULD.
DITTO. I USED THE BOOK EXCUSE TO GET OUT OF THE HOUSE.
AND WE'RE GLAD YOU'RE OKAY.
SERIOUSLY, I'M GLAD TO SEE YOU GUYS.
WOW, I'M SHOCKED THAT THE ONLY THING BROKEN IS YOUR WEB-SHOOTER.
I'LL REPAIR IT WHILE YOU TAKE A BREATHER.
REALLY, DUDE? "I'M SHOCKED..."
I FIGURED MY PUN WENT OVER YOUR HEADS.
THIS IS HIS WAY OF PUNISHING US.
WHERE ARE WE GOING? SHOULDN'T WE SEARCH FOR THE BAD GUY?
TIMES SQUARE. HE'LL NEED TIME TO UNCLOG HIS ARMOR, AND THAT GIVES US A MOMENT TO FIGURE OUT HIS NEXT MOVE.
NOTHING ON THE NEWS OR POLICE FEEDS. SO, WHY TIMES SQUARE?
THERE'S A PERFECT VANTAGE POINT WITHIN WALKING DISTANCE.
WE CAN OBSERVE MAJOR SECTIONS OF THE CITY WHILE I FIX GWEN'S GADGET.
SOUNDS LIKE A PLAN... YOU HUNGRY TOO?
STARVING. YOUR LITTLE EARTHQUAKE SAVED ME FROM DINNER LEFTOVERS FOR BREAKFAST.
AND I HAVE SOME THEORIES I WANT TO SHARE WITH--
SIGH TALKING TO MYSELF AGAIN.

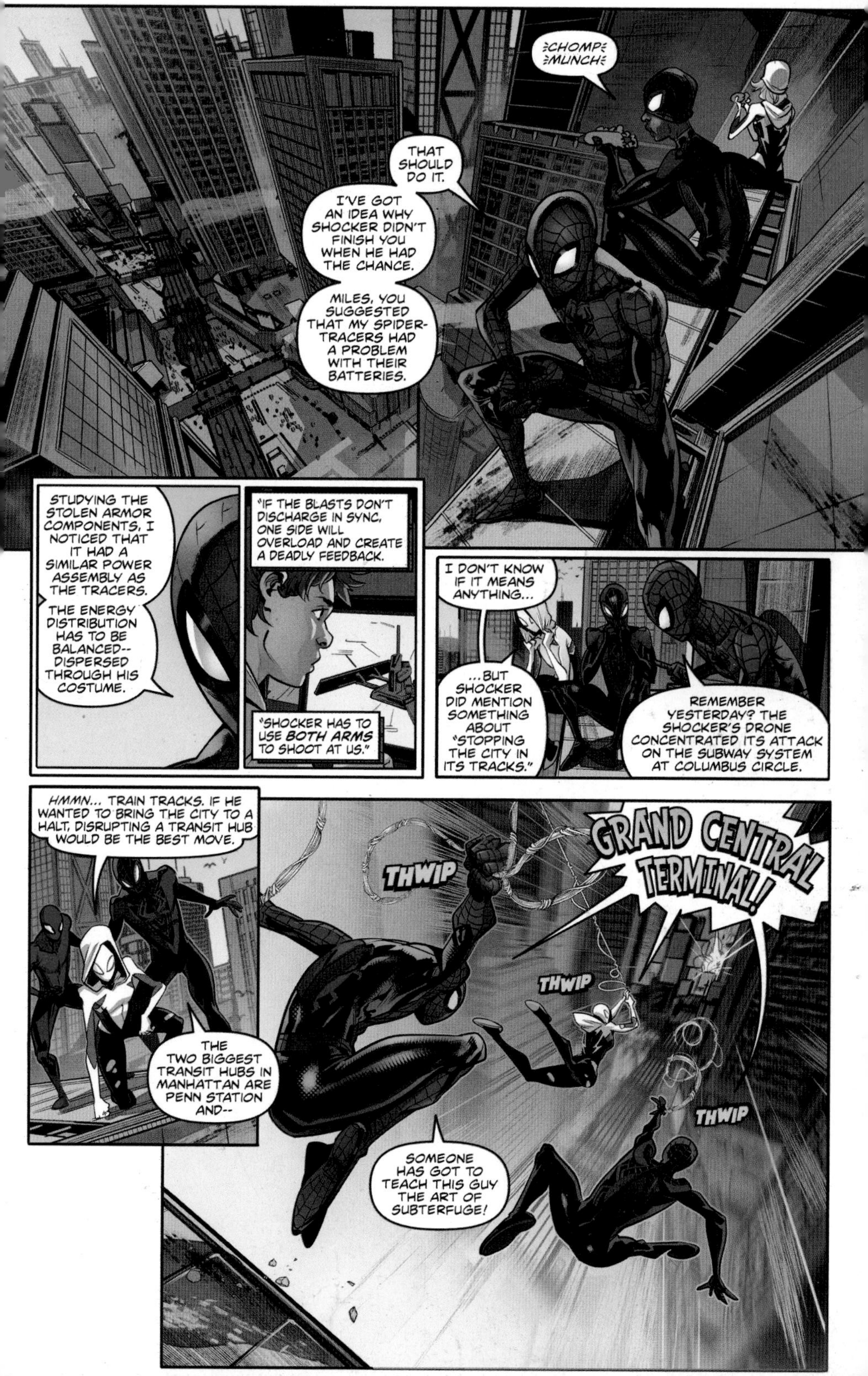

CHOMP MUNCH
THAT SHOULD DO IT.
I'VE GOT AN IDEA WHY SHOCKER DIDN'T FINISH YOU WHEN HE HAD THE CHANCE.
MILES, YOU SUGGESTED THAT MY SPIDER-TRACERS HAD A PROBLEM WITH THEIR BATTERIES.
STUDYING THE STOLEN ARMOR COMPONENTS, I NOTICED THAT IT HAD A SIMILAR POWER ASSEMBLY AS THE TRACERS.
THE ENERGY DISTRIBUTION HAS TO BE BALANCED-- DISPERSED THROUGH HIS COSTUME.
"IF THE BLASTS DON'T DISCHARGE IN SYNC, ONE SIDE WILL OVERLOAD AND CREATE A DEADLY FEEDBACK.
"SHOCKER HAS TO USE BOTH ARMS TO SHOOT AT US."
I DON'T KNOW IF IT MEANS ANYTHING...
...BUT SHOCKER DID MENTION SOMETHING ABOUT "STOPPING THE CITY IN ITS TRACKS."
REMEMBER YESTERDAY? THE SHOCKER'S DRONE CONCENTRATED ITS ATTACK ON THE SUBWAY SYSTEM AT COLUMBUS CIRCLE.
HMMN... TRAIN TRACKS. IF HE WANTED TO BRING THE CITY TO A HALT, DISRUPTING A TRANSIT HUB WOULD BE THE BEST MOVE.
THE TWO BIGGEST TRANSIT HUBS IN MANHATTAN ARE PENN STATION AND--
GRAND CENTRAL TERMINAL!
THWIP
THWIP
THWIP
SOMEONE HAS GOT TO TEACH THIS GUY THE ART OF SUBTERFUGE!

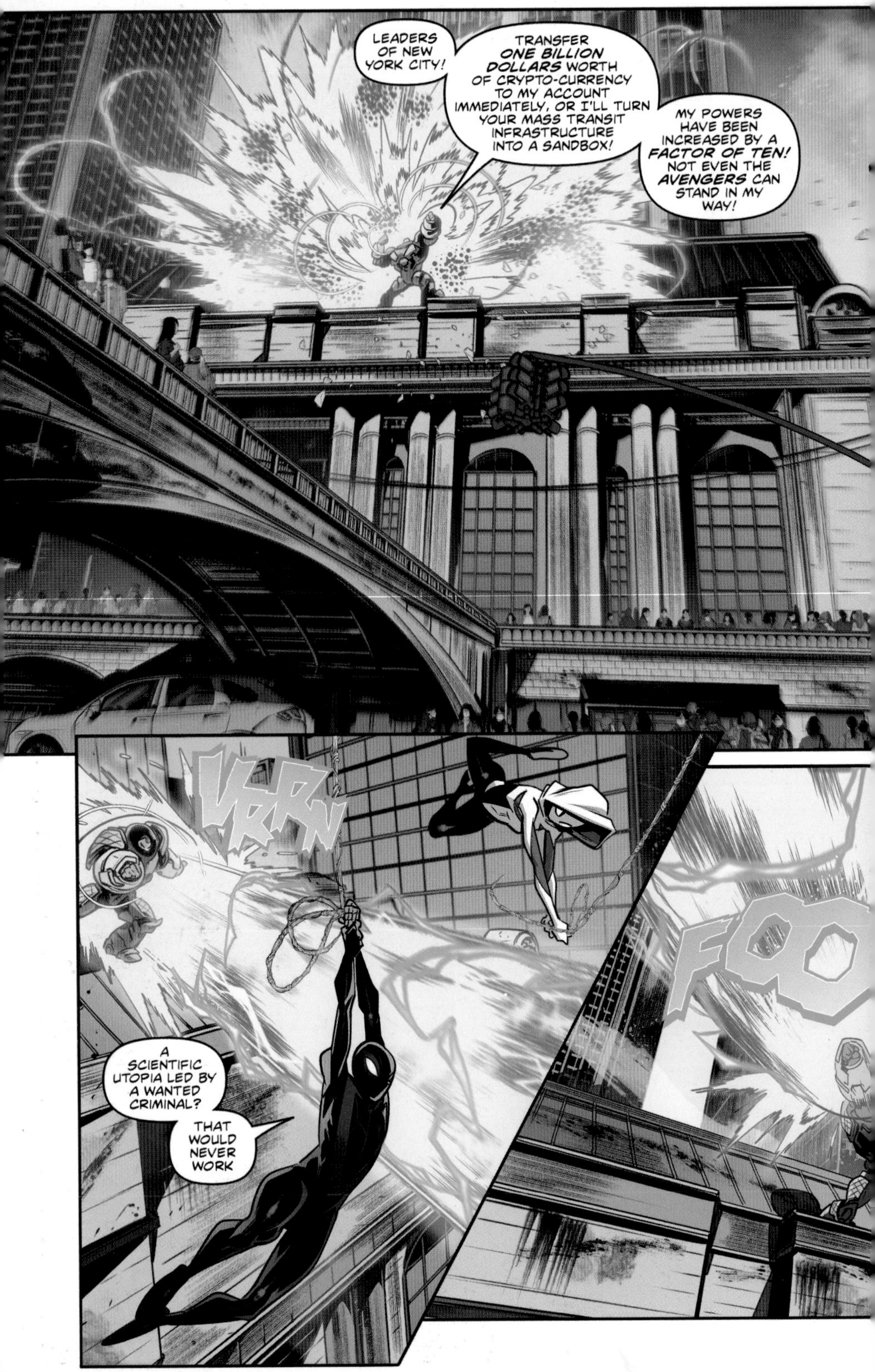
LEADERS OF NEW YORK CITY!
TRANSFER ONE BILLION DOLLARS WORTH OF CRYPTO-CURRENCY TO MY ACCOUNT IMMEDIATELY, OR I'LL TURN YOUR MASS TRANSIT INFRASTRUCTURE INTO A SANDBOX!
MY POWERS HAVE BEEN INCREASED BY A FACTOR OF TEN! NOT EVEN THE AVENGERS CAN STAND IN MY WAY!
VRRN
FOO
A SCIENTIFIC UTOPIA LED BY A WANTED CRIMINAL?
THAT WOULD NEVER WORK

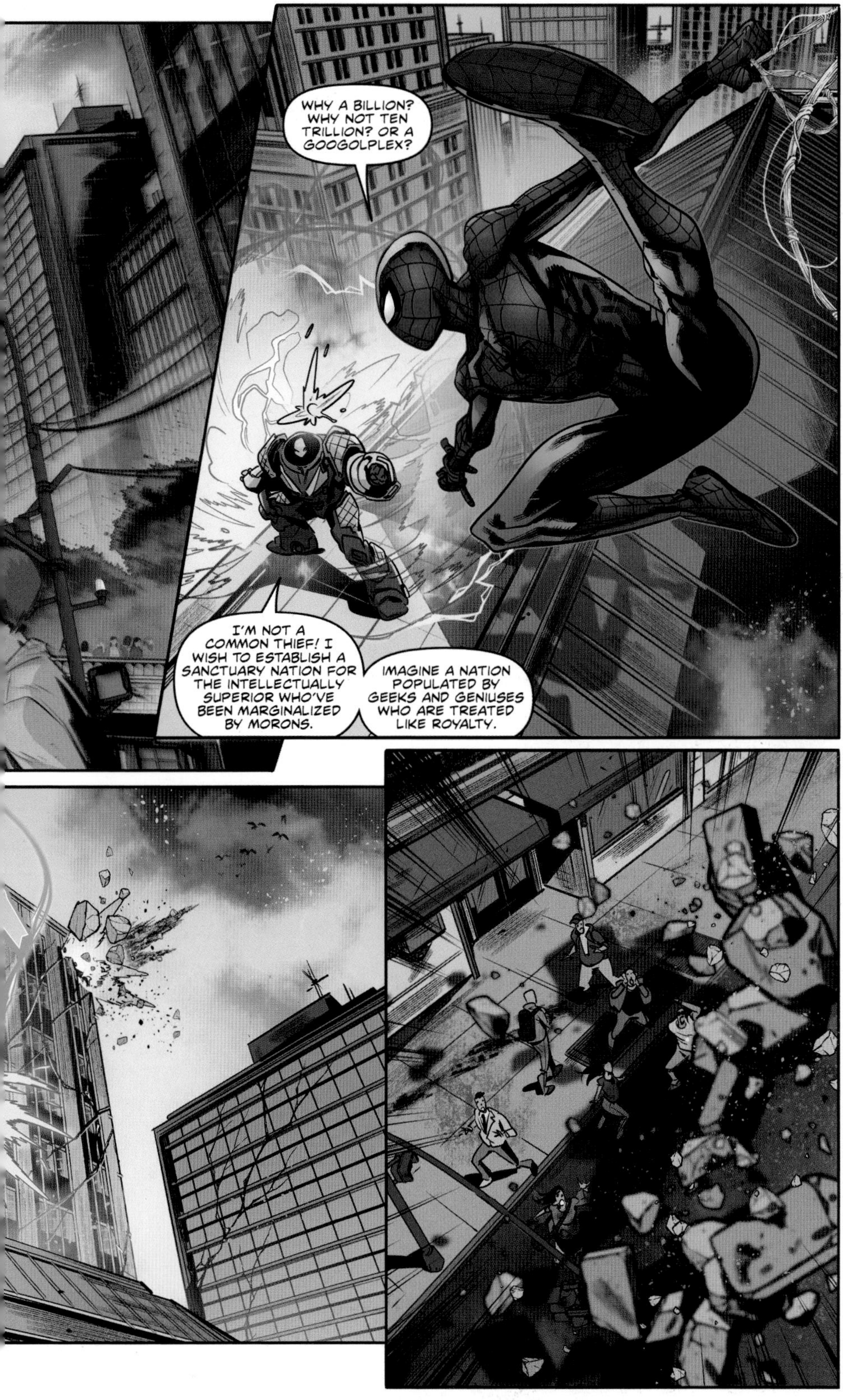
WHY A BILLION? WHY NOT TEN TRILLION? OR A GOOGOLPLEX?
I'M NOT A COMMON THIEF! I WISH TO ESTABLISH A SANCTUARY NATION FOR THE INTELLECTUALLY SUPERIOR WHO'VE BEEN MARGINALIZED BY MORONS.
IMAGINE A NATION POPULATED BY GEEKS AND GENIUSES WHO ARE TREATED LIKE ROYALTY.

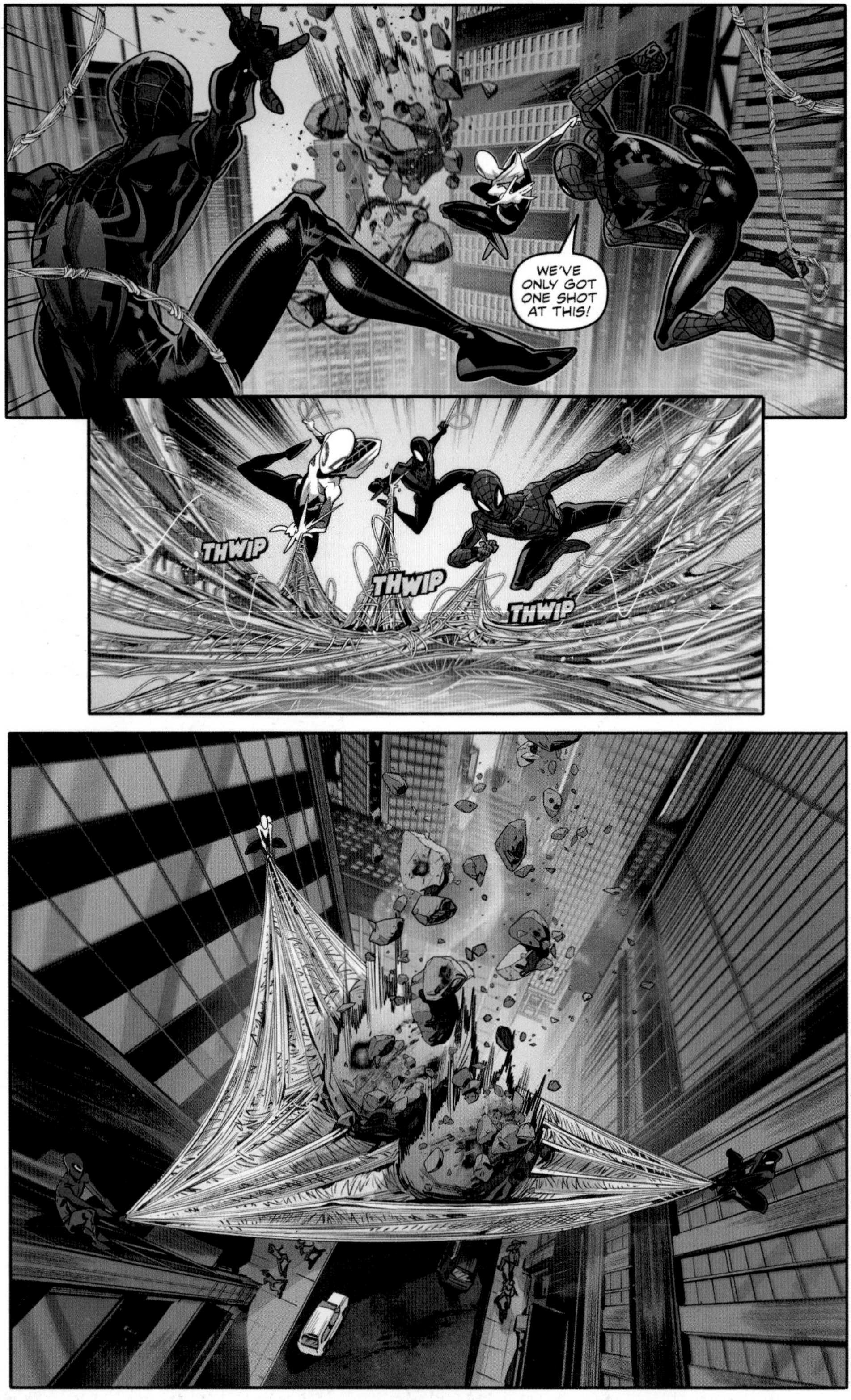
WE'VE ONLY GOT ONE SHOT AT THIS!
THWIP
THWIP
THWIP

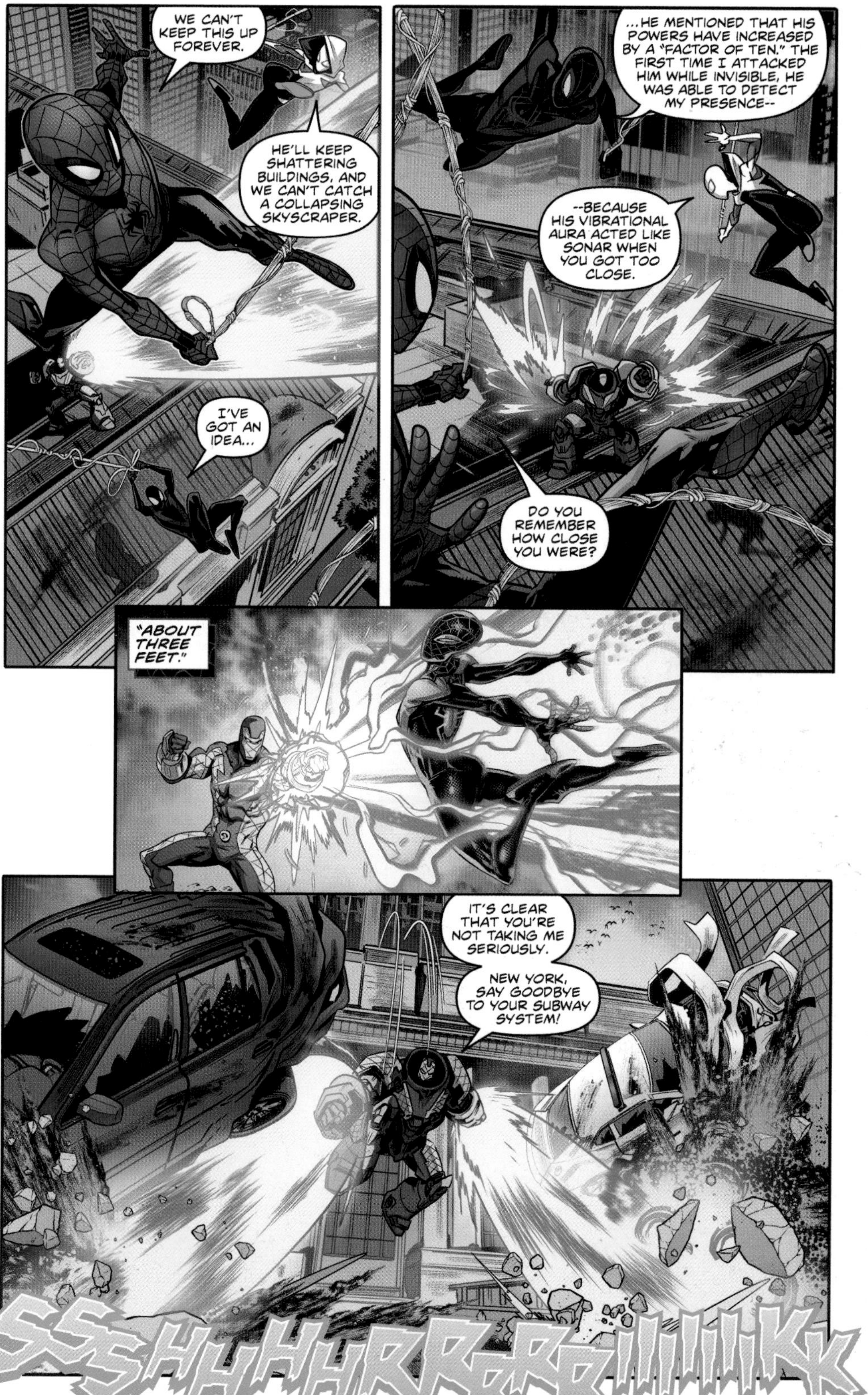
WE CAN'T KEEP THIS UP FOREVER.
HE'LL KEEP SHATTERING BUILDINGS, AND WE CAN'T CATCH A COLLAPSING SKYSCRAPER.
I'VE GOT AN IDEA...
...HE MENTIONED THAT HIS POWERS HAVE INCREASED BY A "FACTOR OF TEN." THE FIRST TIME I ATTACKED HIM WHILE INVISIBLE, HE WAS ABLE TO DETECT MY PRESENCE--
--BECAUSE HIS VIBRATIONAL AURA ACTED LIKE SONAR WHEN YOU GOT TOO CLOSE.
DO YOU REMEMBER HOW CLOSE YOU WERE?
"ABOUT THREE FEET."
IT'S CLEAR THAT YOU'RE NOT TAKING ME SERIOUSLY.
NEW YORK, SAY GOODBYE TO YOUR SUBWAY SYSTEM!
SSSHHHHRRRRRIIIIIIKK

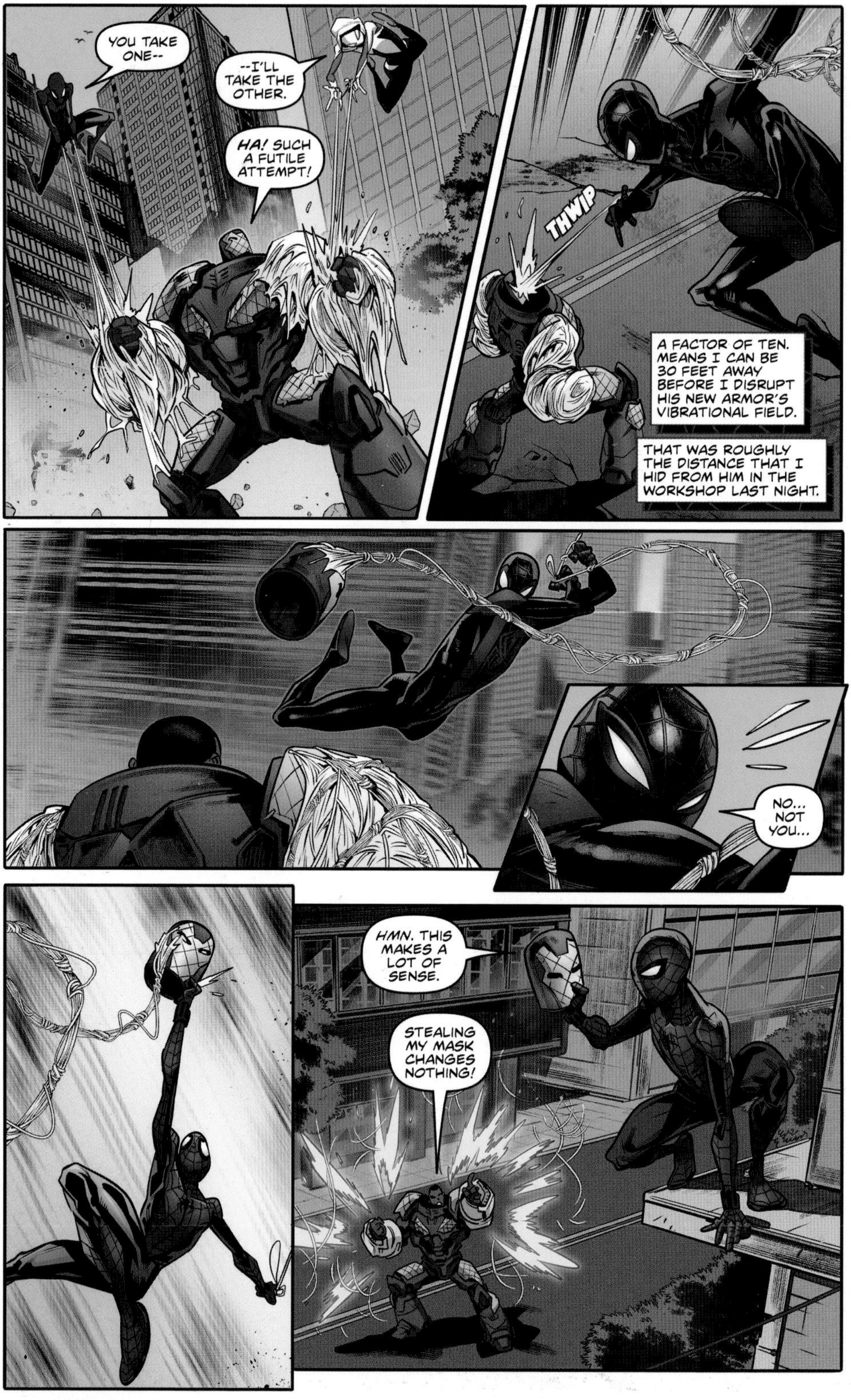
YOU TAKE ONE--
--I'LL TAKE THE OTHER.
HA! SUCH A FUTILE ATTEMPT!
THWIP
A FACTOR OF TEN. MEANS I CAN BE 30 FEET AWAY BEFORE I DISRUPT HIS NEW ARMOR'S VIBRATIONAL FIELD.
THAT WAS ROUGHLY THE DISTANCE THAT I HID FROM HIM IN THE WORKSHOP LAST NIGHT.
NO... NOT YOU...
HMN. THIS MAKES A LOT OF SENSE.
STEALING MY MASK CHANGES NOTHING!

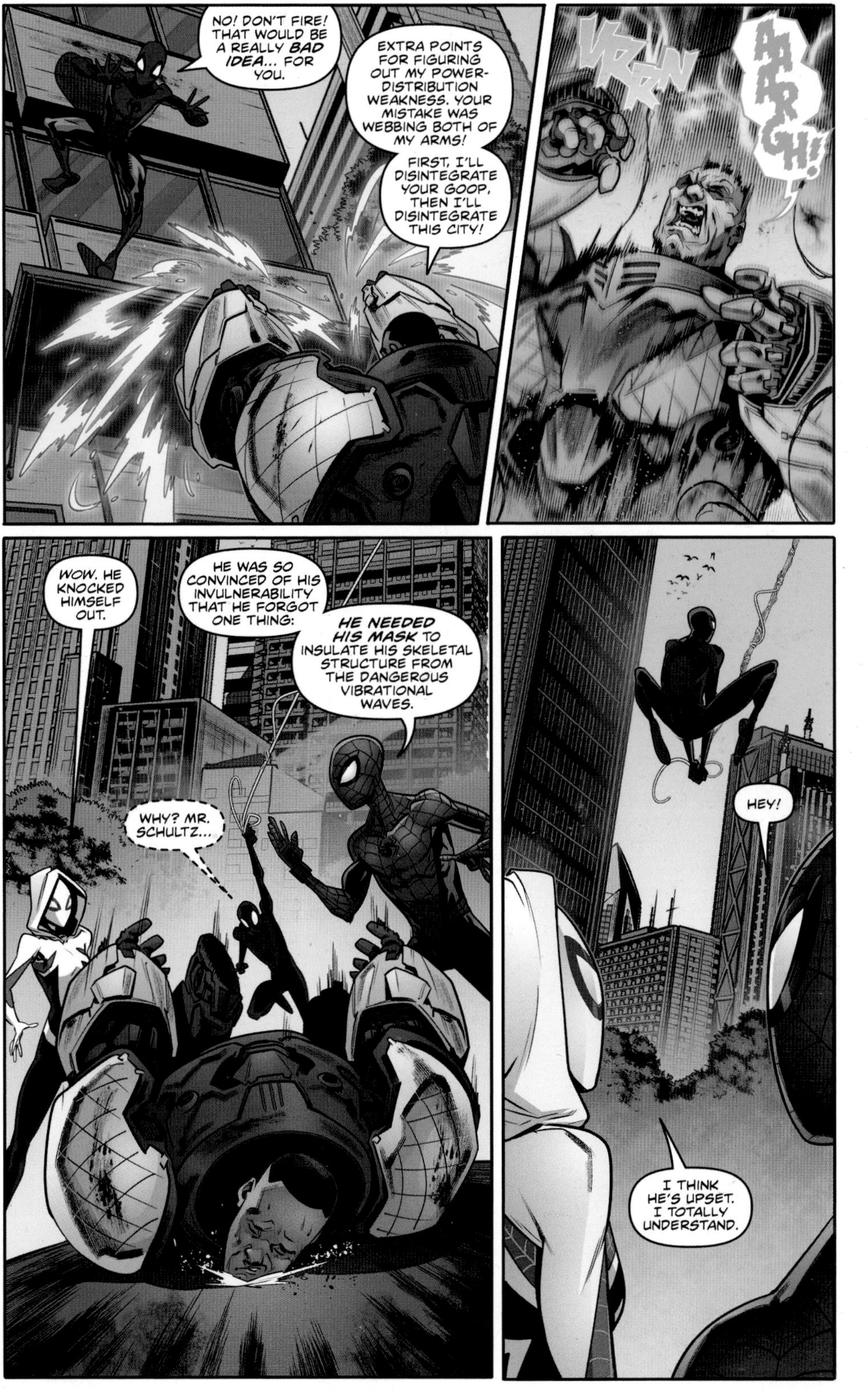
NO! DON'T FIRE! THAT WOULD BE A REALLY BAD IDEA... FOR YOU.
EXTRA POINTS FOR FIGURING OUT MY POWER-DISTRIBUTION WEAKNESS. YOUR MISTAKE WAS WEBBING BOTH OF MY ARMS!
FIRST, I'LL DISINTEGRATE YOUR GOOP, THEN I'LL DISINTEGRATE THIS CITY!
VRRN
AAARGH!
WOW. HE KNOCKED HIMSELF OUT.
HE WAS SO CONVINCED OF HIS INVULNERABILITY THAT HE FORGOT ONE THING:
HE NEEDED HIS MASK TO INSULATE HIS SKELETAL STRUCTURE FROM THE DANGEROUS VIBRATIONAL WAVES.
WHY? MR. SCHULTZ...
HEY!
I THINK HE'S UPSET. I TOTALLY UNDERSTAND.

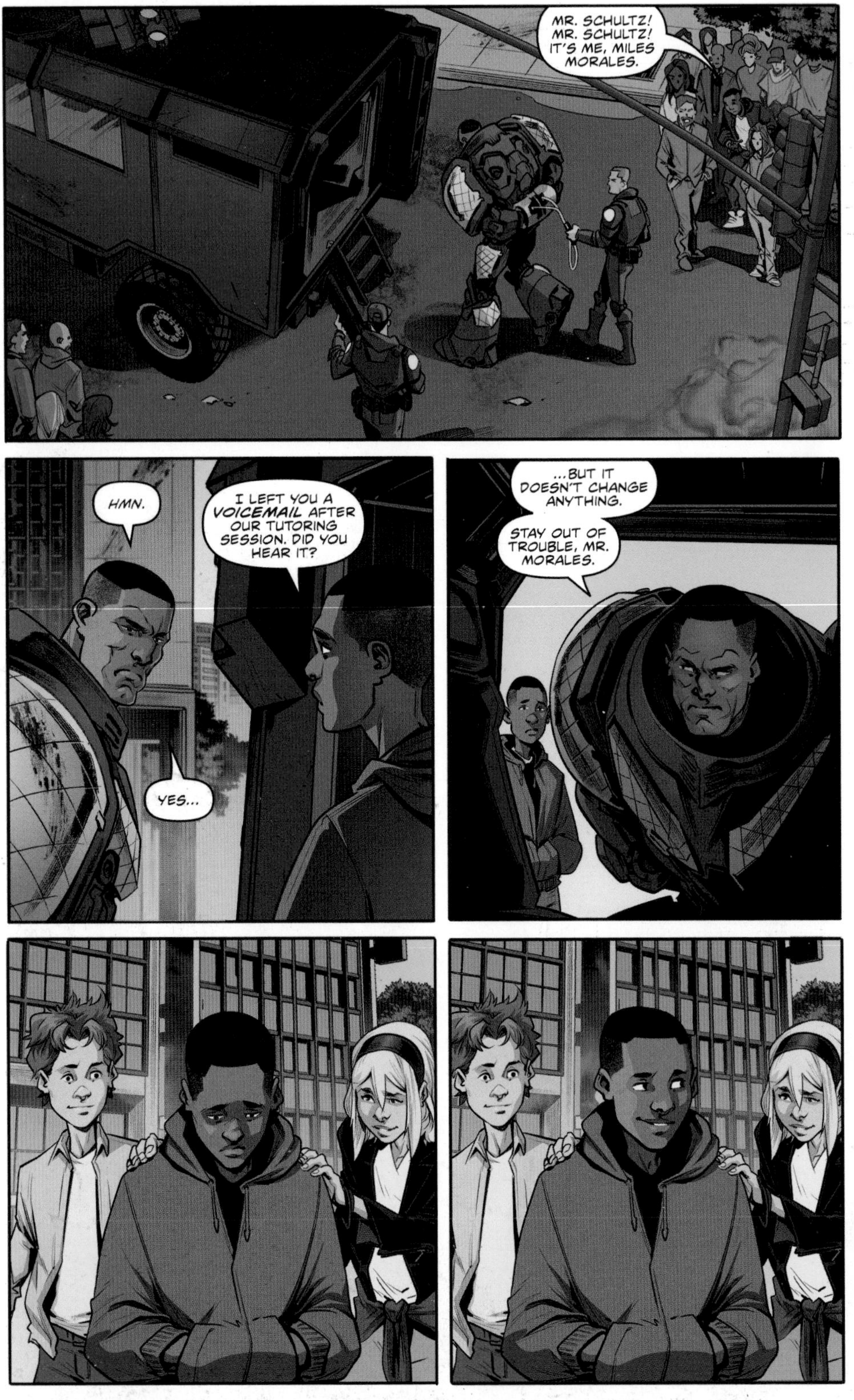
MR. SCHULTZ! MR. SCHULTZ! IT'S ME, MILES MORALES.
HMN.
I LEFT YOU A VOICEMAIL AFTER OUR TUTORING SESSION. DID YOU HEAR IT?
YES...
...BUT IT DOESN'T CHANGE ANYTHING.
STAY OUT OF TROUBLE, MR. MORALES.

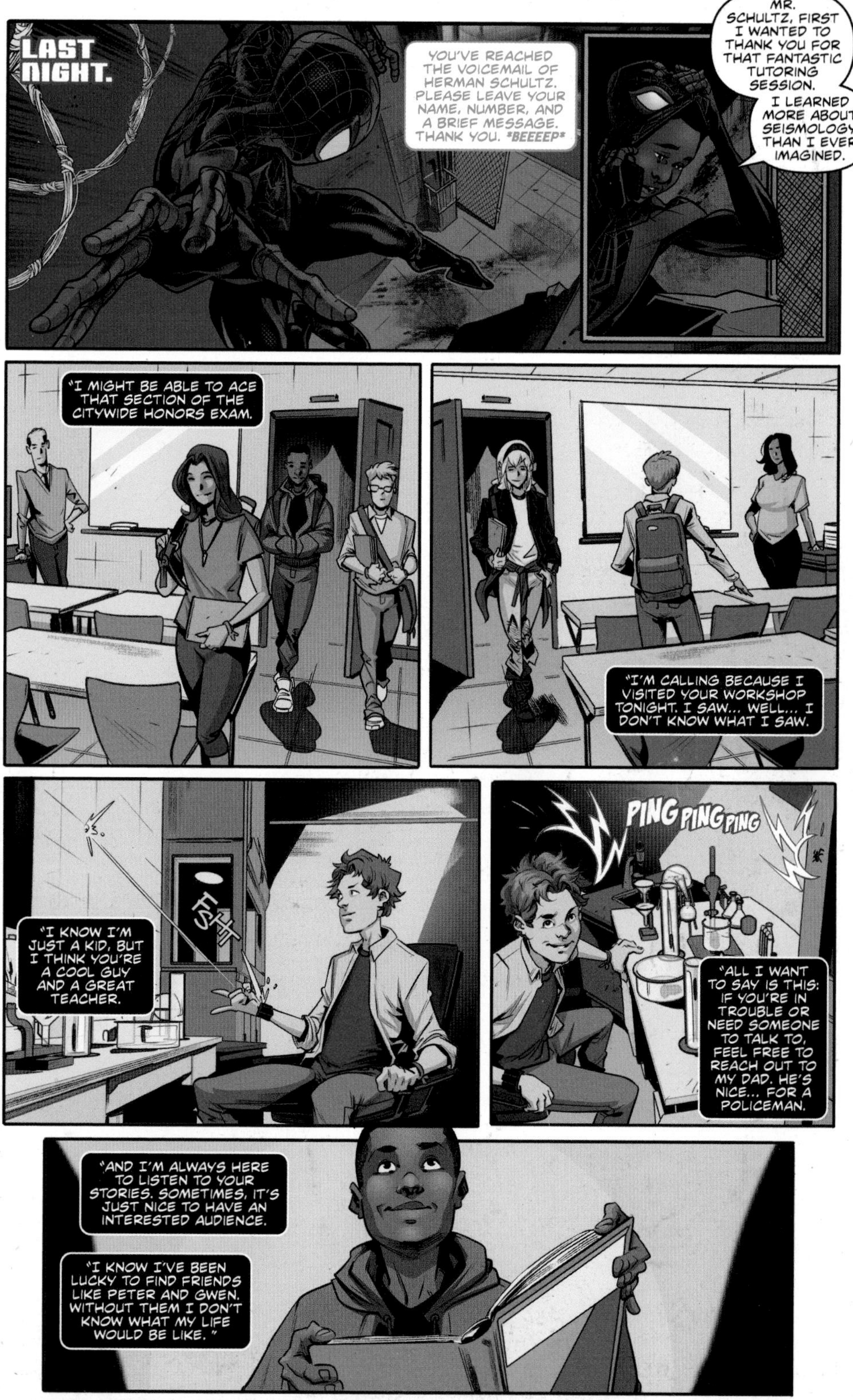
LAST NIGHT.
YOU'VE REACHED THE VOICEMAIL OF HERMAN SCHULTZ. PLEASE LEAVE YOUR NAME, NUMBER, AND A BRIEF MESSAGE. THANK YOU. *BEEEEP*
MR. SCHULTZ, FIRST I WANTED TO THANK YOU FOR THAT FANTASTIC TUTORING SESSION.
I LEARNED MORE ABOUT SEISMOLOGY THAN I EVER IMAGINED.
"I MIGHT BE ABLE TO ACE THAT SECTION OF THE CITYWIDE HONORS EXAM.
"I'M CALLING BECAUSE I VISITED YOUR WORKSHOP TONIGHT. I SAW... WELL... I DON'T KNOW WHAT I SAW.
"I KNOW I'M JUST A KID, BUT I THINK YOU'RE A COOL GUY AND A GREAT TEACHER.
PING PING PING
"ALL I WANT TO SAY IS THIS: IF YOU'RE IN TROUBLE OR NEED SOMEONE TO TALK TO, FEEL FREE TO REACH OUT TO MY DAD. HE'S NICE... FOR A POLICEMAN.
"AND I'M ALWAYS HERE TO LISTEN TO YOUR STORIES. SOMETIMES, IT'S JUST NICE TO HAVE AN INTERESTED AUDIENCE.
"I KNOW I'VE BEEN LUCKY TO FIND FRIENDS LIKE PETER AND GWEN. WITHOUT THEM I DON'T KNOW WHAT MY LIFE WOULD BE LIKE."

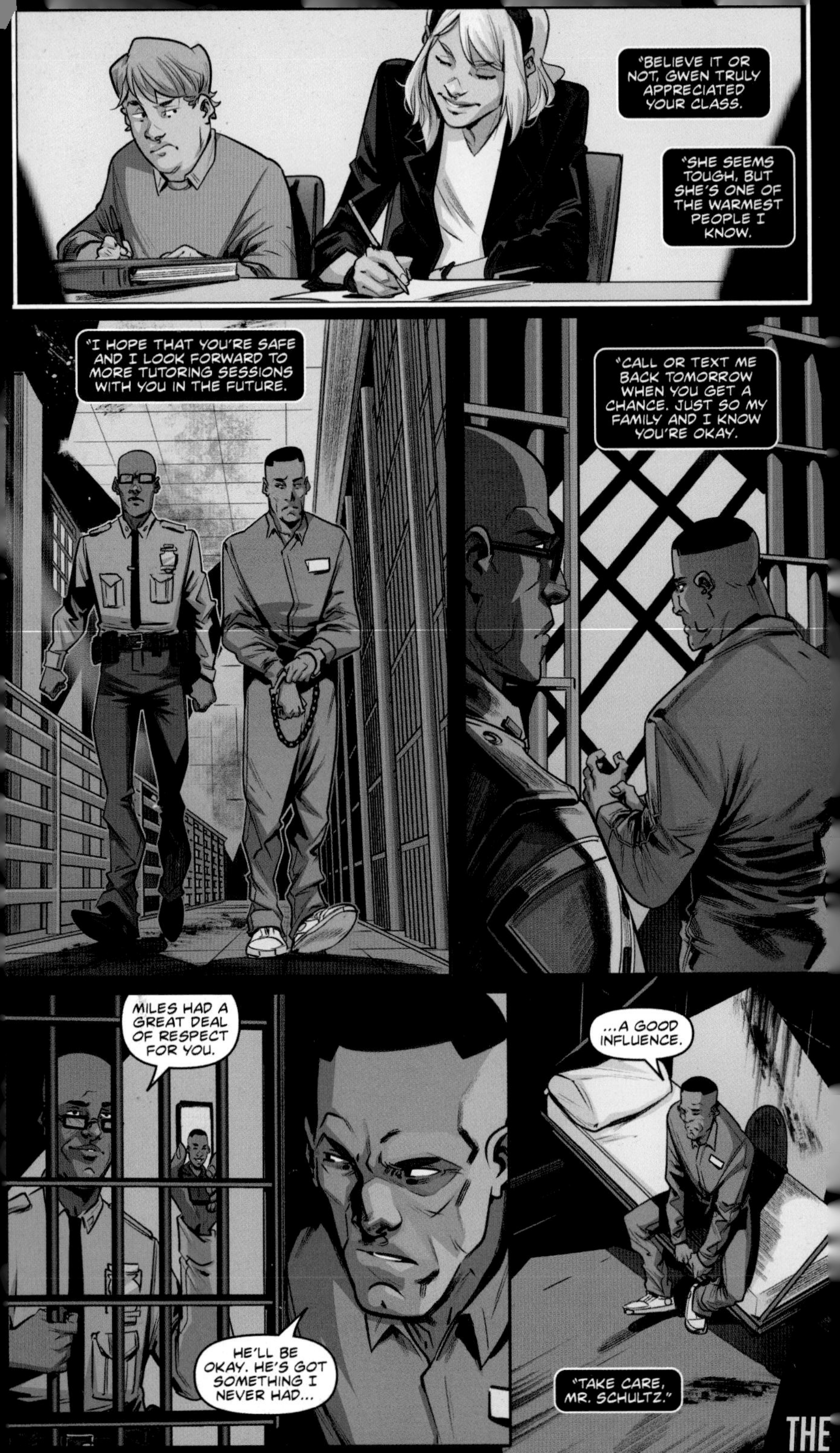
"BELIEVE IT OR NOT, GWEN TRULY APPRECIATED YOUR CLASS.
"SHE SEEMS TOUGH, BUT SHE'S ONE OF THE WARMEST PEOPLE I KNOW.
"I HOPE THAT YOU'RE SAFE AND I LOOK FORWARD TO MORE TUTORING SESSIONS WITH YOU IN THE FUTURE.
"CALL OR TEXT ME BACK TOMORROW WHEN YOU GET A CHANCE. JUST SO MY FAMILY AND I KNOW YOU'RE OKAY.
MILES HAD A GREAT DEAL OF RESPECT FOR YOU.
HE'LL BE OKAY. HE'S GOT SOMETHING I NEVER HAD...
...A GOOD INFLUENCE.
"TAKE CARE, MR. SCHULTZ."
THE

ART BY: **SANFORD GREENE**